WINK @ LIFE

52 AMUSING MUSINGS

Langdon Reid

PUBLISHED BY

WINK AT LIFE

52 AMUSING MUSINGS

PUBLISHED BY: REID PARTNERSHIP

P.O. BOX 2834
STAUNTON, VA 24402

ISBN 978-0-9914544-1-9

Printed in the United States

Cover design & illustrations:
aaron tinsley

This book is dedicated to Alexis, Caroline and Davis.

You three make me who I am.

THE MENU

INTRODUCTION

Hello, my name is Langdon Reid.

PREFACE

I'm only including a Preface in this book because, well, because most books I've read have them and I don't want this one to feel left out. I thought about calling this the Preamble because, well, quite frankly, this is the part of this book where I'm writing something before I officially start to "amble" on with my thoughts and musings. But there's really only just one Preamble and no matter how insightful and awesome my preamble would be, it could still never stand up or even compete with THE Preamble. A lot like naming a child Elvis. No matter how great and influential he may grow up to be, there is only and will always be just one Elvis. So I won't call this section a preamble if you won't name your kid Elvis. Deal?

This is a collection of columns I've written over the past few years. Some are funny. Some are serious. Some are meaningful. And some are completely purposeless. But one thing I strive for in my writings is that they all are relatable. I strive to write a wholesome, relatable column with everyday familiar topics that are addressed with concern, morality, and sincerity along with a humorous and sometimes sardonic slant that will leave the reader with a smile.

I like to think of myself as a professional Observationalist. (I think the correct term is just Observer, but Observationalist sounds like it should pay more.) I enjoy people and what makes them who they are. And why they do the things they do. And say the things they say.

And dress the way they dress. You get the point. People, and the way they live their lives, intrigue me. And I tend to think that we all share some of these same idiosyncrasies that ultimately make us the most complex, interesting and compelling creatures around.

I'm not here to change anyone, point my finger in judgment, slide in an agenda or make you believe the same things I do. I'm just here to weigh in with an observant eye and a colorful pen and to shoot straight with you. In other words, I'm just winking at life.

All of these columns have been published, however, they are appearing in this book completely unedited. Sometimes a piece will get edited at the last minute by the editor, usually because of column space limits. And keep in mind that obviously, some of these pieces were written according to certain events and situations happening in the world at the time.

A tip of the hat and many thanks to my hometown newspaper, The News Leader, for originally publishing these columns. A big high five to Aaron Tinsley, for his creative eye and artistic pen to bring some of these words to pictures and for an awesome cover. And most importantly, I do want to thank all of you for your kind words and comments on these writings---especially the words of encouragement. They mean a lot and I sincerely appreciate them. And those words of encouragement are the very reason for me putting this book together. I enjoy writing and it's obvious you enjoy reading. And I hope you'll enjoy reading these as much as I enjoyed writing them.

BAGELS & SPEED BUMPS

With the experience and knowledge I've gained throughout my multiple summers here upon this earth, I have discovered that two minor changes need to take place in our daily routines that will deliver us from the inevitable stress and frustration that ultimately leads to, well, more stress and frustration. Oh yeah, this is assuming, of course, that your daily routine is the same as mine!

Okay, here's the first one. You see, my mornings go pretty good, all things considered, except when it comes to breakfast. I have noticed that people who eat a healthy quick breakfast, would eat something like a grapefruit or a granola bar or worse yet, an undersized oat-bran mini-muffin with that irritating spray butter that after you've developed carpel tunnel from violently pumping your trigger finger, it barely gets your muffin damp! No sir, not me. I need something with a little more substance to start clogging my arteries first thing in the morning.

So, after being scolded by health headlines proclaiming that breakfast *is* the most important meal of the day, I decided to compromise my cholesterol level for some kind of breakfast item that could attempt to also somewhat satiate my taste buds. So, I went to the bagel. I do refuse to toast it, because I'll never accept the idea that everybody *loves* soft warm bread but then they'll turn right around and put that puppy in the toaster and after the charred edges have cut the roof of their mouths, they'll still insist that it's delicious. You ain't foolin' me, people!

But here's where I encounter my first frustration of the day. It's the half-cut bagel. The bagel is only partially cut. It doesn't even qualify as a "cut"; actually it's more of a "perforation." I mean, is there some little guy sitting in the Thomas' Bagel Plant who is trained to only cut the bagel, but not all the way? No, apparently the Thomases want us to pry and break the bagel apart with our hands, which winds up looking more like a strangling maneuver, which results in leaving a badly bruised bagel sitting on top of a plate full of bagel crumbs! And you can't cut it, either, because you're concentrating on trying to match your cut with the little bagel guy's perforation, and then you get off track and then you've just introduced yourself to a whole 'nother set of issues. And don't go try the English Muffins, 'cause they're the same way! You just have to cut them on the left side.

And to add to my frustration throughout the day, enter the speed bump. I'd love to have just five minutes in a room with the guy who came up with this brilliant idea. And we're being *attacked* by speed bumps, too. They're everywhere! Grocery stores, parks, factories, banks, malls, strip malls, antique strip malls, comic strip malls---you name it, they're there. Obviously, I realize that their purpose is to slow the driver down for the safety of the pedestrian. But when I'm drinking my coffee and go over one these little mountains, my concentration is now spent on negotiating my coffee in mid-air with no regard to any pedestrian that may be impeding my immediate traffic pattern. Pedestrian safety is gone out the window, pal; my only concern is not scolding my inner thighs and contemplating another "coffee-lap lawsuit."

And then, like it wasn't annoying enough to start with, somebody decided to put the speed bumps at an angle. So now, your entire car rocks ferociously enough that you can actually bang your head against the window and knock yourself unconscious while driving. Oh yeah, that's smart. About as smart as a cargo basket on a pogo stick!

I'll say this much: speed bumps do slow the car in motion down. (Then why don't we call them slow bumps? 'Cause we don't speed over them; we go slower over them!) However, the rage the driver experiences that is brought on by the speed bump is more harmful and impending to the pedestrian than the intended purpose of the speed bump.

So if we could do away with half-cut bagels and those six-inch speed bumps, we're on our way to a happier, stress-free, less frustrating life of blissful living. 'Cause one thing's for sure: I ain't gonna start eating one of them puny healthy grapefruits for breakfast!

LIVIN' IN AN ABB. WRLD.

I am watching ESPN on TV in HD while syncing my PDA up to my PC. We live in one big abbreviated world. I can't remember the last time I talked to someone and the conversation wasn't peppered with abbreviated words and acronyms galore. I'm all for shortcuts and concepts that get things done quicker, however, only if the meaning of what is being said or done is not compromised in the process. Case in point, I asked a 17-year old the other day what PDA stood for and he froze. "I don't know what it stands for---I just know what it is." In his defense, I'm sure he probably knew how to break down the motherboard and put it back together and that's a lot more useful than knowing what three little letters stand for. (Btw, it stands for Personal Digital Assistant. Not Public Display of Affection!)

But I still tend to take issue with somebody if they only know the "call letters" and not what they stand for. And I speak on this from being guilty of this very thing a long time ago. I was asked what ESPN stood for and I had no idea. I've watched ESPN since its inception, which is most of my life. I couldn't even make up something believable on the spot. I looked like a fool. Therefore, lesson learned. (In my defense and to be unnecessarily technical, ESPN used to stand for Entertainment & Sports Programming Network, but shortly thereafter the official name became just the four letters, now, standing for nothing. Much like

9

President Truman's middle name! And you never even knew President Truman watched ESPN.)

It's no big secret that the constant introductions of advanced technologies contribute the most to our big ol' sea of abbreviations. We've got VCR, DVD, Email, JPEG, HDMI cables, SIM cards, RAM, PCS, .com, IBM, IBS, and I B Stupid. Don't even get me started on the stock market ticker scrolling across the bottom of my TV. A lot of those symbols have no relevance or relation whatsoever to the company they're representing. I thought my portfolio had gone up 20%---come to find out I was watching the wrong symbols and wound up in the wrong joke!

Since we've already had Generation X and now Generation Next, then the upcoming one has got to be Generation Text. Emailing began popularizing the art of shortcuts and abbreviating, but texting has taken it to a whole new level. I used to have to diagram sentences in school but this generation is going to struggle to recognize a complete sentence. The heck with subjects and predicates, a colorful adjective and a transitive verb--- they're speaking in fragments! I do text but I'm hurtin' over here. I'm still disappointed there's not a SpellCheck option on my phone. I'm worrying too much about my texts being free of dangling participles and that the antecedents agree. I'm trying to keep up, though.

I'll leave you with this story. Recently I was in a meeting discussing some options concerning music business and the abbreviated jargon was running wild. At one point, this is the sentence I heard from the man sitting behind the ornate mahogany desk. *I talked to the A & R at BMI and he can 86 the ser. charge with a group comp. and if there's a co-pub on a demo, they can admin the royalties for you.* What?! I had no idea what this guy was saying to me---

I just told him to get in touch with my people. Now I just need to go find some people.

So with all this being said, one more question: Ever wondered why 'abbreviation' is such a long word? Oh, the irony.

SPEECH ACCEPTANCES

"I would like to thank the Academy..." Yadda yadda yeah yeah. Whatever. Newsflash: At this point of the show, nobody is listening to your list of thank yous. We could really care less who is on this deserving list because we are too busy grading your wardrobe and hairstyle. We can't help it; it's just the way we judgmental animals are wired. It's the same reason we care more about the red carpet portion than the Best Picture. We tune in to see what skimpy dress Jennifer Lopez is falling out of this year but yet can't stay awake to see if some sci-fi movie about the Smurfs with their own language took home top honors.

It hit me the other night while watching the Oscars that we enjoy guessing who will win, then enjoy seeing the winner's reaction and we *want* to enjoy his or her acceptance speech but, so often, they let us down. They start by thanking the Academy, which is understandable since they're the ones who brought them to the dance. And then they move on to their agent; this is known as job security as you want to keep this guy on your side. But then they start listing off production assistants, second key grips, their veterinarian, yoga instructor, right down to the caterer's nephew. All because they are so scared they might leave somebody out. It's a sensitive gesture but the overkill quickly moves me into the "I don't care" category really fast.

I enjoy listening to stories, sermons, maybe even an interesting lecture from time to time, but you have to grab me quick if I'm staying with you on the entire 40-second thank you nods. First of all, don't you think they need to be prepared? Preparation is the first main ingredient. I mean how long have they known that there is a one in five chance that they might win? Those are pretty good odds. You don't have to type it all up on a scroll as long as Santa's naughty list, but don't they remember lines for a living? That's one of the reasons they are standing on that stage; they are really good at remembering lines! And please whatever you do don't pull out a piece of paper. As soon as we see an index card emerge from the left breast pocket of a tuxedo, millions of eyes roll across the country.

Or what about when the screenwriter wins and he gets up there and admits he doesn't know what to say. You just wrote an entire movie! You can't write a 30 second speech?

Speaking of long speeches, the longest on record was given by Greer Garson in 1942 when she won Best Actress. She rambled, excuse me, I mean talked for five and a half minutes. She sealed her fate that night---she never won again.

Best Supporting Actress Maureen Stapleton candidly stated, "I want to thank...everybody I ever met in my entire life." The brush doesn't get much broader than that.

For playing a mute character in *Johnny Belinda*, Jane Wyman said, "I accept this very gratefully for keeping my mouth shut for once. I think I'll do it again." Now that's clever.

And Sir Laurence Olivier made audiences squirm with his nonsensical display of poetic prattle when he referenced "the great firmament" and "the euphoria that happens to so many of us at the first breath of the majestic glow of a new tomorrow." And your point is?

The second main ingredient is emotion. It has to be sincere and heartfelt, but not over the top. Be grateful but humble. It's an honor so make sure it's treated that way.

And one more thing: please don't get political. I don't want my politicians to act nor my actors to politicize. It's just unnecessary and it makes us all uncomfortable.

My favorite acceptance speech? 1968. The Irving Thalberg Memorial Award at the Academy Awards. Alfred Hitchcock. He walked to podium, received his little gold bust and politely said, "Thank you." Then walked away. Thank you, Mr. Hitchcock.

AMERICA'S PASTIME

I was last Saturday much pleased in witnessing a company of active young men playing the manly and athletic game of "base ball." Any person fond of witnessing this game may avail himself of seeing it played with consummate skill and wonderful dexterity...it is innocent amusement, and healthy exercise, attended with but little expense, and has no demoralizing tendency.

This is part of a letter that appeared in a New York newspaper, *National Advocate*, in 1823, sixteen years *before* the game was reportedly invented by Abner Doubleday. Obviously, cut-throat agents hadn't contaminated the sport with over-inflated contracts and the desire to hit a longer homer by juiced up pectoral giants hadn't come in to play: other than that, it's a wonderful description of America's pastime for the first time.

So many comforting memories of baseball in my pastime: the smell of an oily glove, the rough feel of stitched seams under two fingers, the amplified clicking of metal cleats on concrete which automatically prompts an arrogant dugout strut, the sight of a freshly mowed outfield contrasting symmetrical rake marks on the infield, and the nervous tastes of salt, dirt, and humidity while standing in the batter's box wondering if it's going to be a slider, low and away, or a fastball, high and tight. The game definitely possesses its own magic.

My childhood sandlot was a backyard wiffle ball game with pizza top boxes for bases and if you powered one far enough to hit the house, then touch 'em all. And if you hit the kitchen window or got it stuck in the gutter, automatic grand slam! There was a 3x4 section on the side of the house outlined in chalk that was desperately losing its mortar due to many late evenings, before and after dinner, throwing a tennis ball at this brick target. And that homemade dirt BMX ramp in the corner of the yard doubled as the perfect pitcher's mound. And for my birthday one year, I got the prized Rod Carew plastic spring action pop-up pedal tee. Place the ball on the small yellow catapult, stomp on the pedal, and swing away! This memory came full circle one day: I'm proud to say that a personal used bat from this Hall of Fame slugger is among my souvenirs.

Let's not forget baseball cards, either. Every kid who has ever been impassioned with the sport, has bought, traded and collected baseball cards. I've always heard about bike riders putting them in their spokes to create that cool motor sound, but not me. I valued mine too much to ruffle up those edges. I've still got that royal blue vinyl case that housed each teams' players in perfect order. The most valuable baseball card to date is a 1909 T206 Honus Wagner. Somebody paid $1.1 million for one ten years ago. That's one expensive piece of colored cardboard right there. A lot of people don't know this, but I have a Honus Wagner, too. Well, actually it's an 8x10 replica of the card that I bought off eBay for $4, but still it's fun to say that I have a framed Wagner in my house!

I still like to drift off to peaceful sleep watching a Major League game. Sometimes I'm lucky enough to dream that I'm 8 years old again, perched behind a wood veneer tv tray holding a blue score book learning how to keep score.

Backward Ks, fielder's choices, double plays, and base hits. I'd put off studying for Spelling tests and learning how to carry the one for accurate double-digit addition, just to sit in front of a 19" Quasar tv filling in dots and drawing base runner lines in the tiny squares of that scorebook. In the margins, I'd keep track of trying to guess what kind of pitch the pitcher would throw next according to the batter and the count. I'd have on my Batman pajamas but also my wobbly plastic batting helmet, the same kind Chris Chambliss wore at bat *and* in the field. And I never understood why I couldn't tuck my jeans down in my socks and wear my multi-colored Astros jersey and carry a rosin bag instead of a book bag so I could look more like Nolan Ryan going to school.

Oh well, I can spell pretty good and can carry the one, but I'm tucking my jeans in and nobody can stop me. So bring it on, let the games begin and let's enjoy the best game America has ever known! Play ball!

ARIZONA SHOOTING: WHY?

It's been a little over two weeks since the shootings that happened in Arizona. Breaking news of investigations and new information and thankful miraculous recoveries fill the headlines daily, as well as the replaying of the tragic event laying heavy on our hearts and minds.

When an event like this happens with fatalities, be it war, school shootings, 9/11, or the recent Arizona shootings, one question always and immediately is the first to be asked; *why*? One small word with three little letters has confounded the most intelligent, logical, faithful, compassionate and understanding minds since the ages began.

This question begs our reason and gnaws at us like a termite through wood. It's rarely ever answered and we are only satisfied once we stop asking it and somewhere deep down find the strength to accept the situation at hand. And by accepting it, I don't mean that we accept it by saying it is okay, but rather accepting the situation given to us in terms of what has happened has happened and how can I make good, right, and healthy from here on out.

We have to look beyond the question and the grief to find solace in the positive amid the tragedy. Among the tears and confusion, I've seen strength and faith and compassion. I've seen prayer and miracles and forgiveness. Often times, a tragic scene is a backdrop to see those beautiful and wonderful things we have in life that we sometimes take for granted or get overlooked.

Six people's lives were taken in the line of duty. 14 more were wounded in their line of duty. And their line of duty was simply living life to its fullest and being the people they were created to be. We all do what we do and Life takes its course around us. And sometimes *through* us. Heroes are born out of ordinary people doing what needs to be done in unpredictable and unusual circumstances. If we just play out the talents and gifts that God has given us, nothing can be determined in the future, and no matter what may happen in the present, only greatness will be left behind. Do what we do to be all that we can be for the time that we are graciously given.

We all feel the direst need to answer the question of "why" to find comfort, relieve guilt and hopefully somehow see a hint of reason that will divert a hurtful situation like this again. We want to know why. We know all the others: the who, what, when, where, and how. But why?

Socrates, one of the wisest of the wise, once said, "Wisdom begins in wonder." This was the same man who was forced to drink poison because his constant questioning really bothered people. It made them think and look deep into themselves to find a better way and maybe even a better person.

So may we continue to question and wonder in the ever hopes to become healthier and better in our lives, but yet stop short in that questioning so it may not destruct us in our own illusive search.

BACKSPACE

I really hope I don't crash while writing this. And I hope my computer doesn't crash either. But if I do, I should be up and back at it in a couple of hours and I know why I crashed: because I didn't get enough sleep last night or I'm coming down with something. However, if my computer crashes, well, I'm never really sure what caused it and exactly how it ever gets back to better.

Living right smack dab in the Age of Technology, we rely and depend on our computers sometimes even more than our friends, family and secretaries. As I write this, I am looking at my keyboard and it's sinking in for the first time that these computer designers and makers of long ago, thought of it all. I was introduced to the computer in the fourth grade, so I know where all the buttons are and how to use them to get done what I need to get done. But to stop and look and realize the importance of each key's purpose and how it applies to the task at hand is quite amazing. The keyboard is patterned after the very "motherboard" that each of us has. Well, almost.

It obviously has all the punctuation marks to inflect our message, and an ALL CAPS button for when we need to shout and *really* get our point across. I like the SHIFT Key because it allows me to multi-task: such as one key that represents the number 4 and the dollar sign ($), but can only be achieved by hitting Shift. The Escape key is fun to use, especially in my life as I can usually just squander up a blank stare, drift off in the other direction and completely escape the situation at hand.

The Control/Alt/Delete function is a favorite. By hitting these three together, you can shut down and refresh and ultimately reset. How many times throughout the day do I need to do this! Sometimes I Control/Alt/Delete myself by closing my eyes and counting to ten and sometimes by propping my feet up and partaking in some peanut butter crackers and a glass of lemonade. Ahhhh...refreshed.

Hands down, my favorite keyboard application in my life is the HOME key. Whether it's calling and checking in or knowing that I'm just a song away from walking in the back door, going home is always good.

But the one key that my keyboard has that I don't have in my life is Backspace. The letters are almost worn off this button because I use it so much. So many times I write something to see how it sounds and after reading it a few different times and a few different ways, I immediately start slamming down on it to erase it completely from the record so that no one may ever know what was written or even thought about it. I tried it, and could see that it wasn't right or good, so it got Backspaced.

But how many times has my tongue worked faster than my filter system in my mind? Or when a thought has been blurted out before it could have been properly structured and formatted? Oh how I wish I had a dress rehearsal for everything I say so it could be crafted just like I'd like it to be. The closest thing to Backspace we have is the word Sorry. We can't take it back; we have to just leave it out there as a reminder that we may not want to do it that way again. On second thought, we *do* have the Backspace key on all of our human keyboards; it's just that it can only be pushed by someone else. It's the "I Forgive You" key. It's the "Don't Worry About It" key. It's the most powerful key we have but can only be applied by, not the actions or choice of ourselves, but rather by the actions and choice of others.

There's a lot I don't understand about my computer but what little I do, I'm gong to try to be more like it. I'm going to do what I can to stay away from viruses and use my Backspace for others as much as I can.

BARRY WHITE RUINED IT FOR ALL OF US GUYS

Didn't I just get you something for Christmas? I know I did because my credit card statement says that I'm still paying for it. It was either a fancy piece of furniture for that room in the house I never go in or an overrated and overpriced small piece of jewelry. And now I'm supposed to bow to the wiles of a little naked baby runnin' around shootin' people in their fluffy buttocks so they may forevermore affirm their undeniable love for one another? Aw c'mon. I ain't buyin' in to this one!

Who is St. Valentine anyway? Well, glad you asked 'cause I did some research. Well, actually I just Wikipedia-ed him and here's what I found out. St. Valentine, or Valentinus, was a saint of some kind or other in ancient Rome. He was really smart and stuff and affected people in a really good way and then those people got together and had a feast in his honor. (There were a lot of dates and big words in the article so it got confusing and I quickly became bored with my in-depth research.) I'm certain his priestly deeds were surely sacrosanct and I wish not to demean those in any way whatsoever, but I did not see where this man left instructions for me to further patronize Russell Stover or go further in debt by purchasing a vase full of flowers that will be dead by the end of the week.

But I did find out one of the culprits in developing this day to how we lovingly know it to be today: Geoffrey

Chaucer. Yep, Mr. Chaucer back in the 1300s decided to write these lines in a poem titled "Parlement of Foules":

For this was on seynt Volantynys day
Whan euery bryd comyth there to chese [chose] his make [mate]

Basically this translates as "go out and buy your Sweet and Lovely something really nice to make her happy so you won't have to crash on the couch tonight." Then the amorous French developed their Highly Court of Love (that's really what it was called!) shortly thereafter, which supported and established law in the favor of women based on the language of poetry. Only the French.

And as if this wasn't enough, then some 570 years later, along came Barry White. Yes, "The Man with the Velvet Voice." "The Sultan of Smooth Soul." "The Walrus of Love." Big Barry wooed the ladies with his romantic and sultry lyrics and declared them with a somewhat lascivious delivery of low notes that could only be found in musical basements. He sold over 50 million records using his bedroom tones flattering the female gender. In the 70s, a candlelit dinner and some B.W. on the phonograph was far better than a lousy folded piece of cardboard asking her to be your valentine. Barry was the harbinger for my Valentine's Day woes yet to come.

Which brings me around to what this day should really be called: Hip Happy Hooray for Hallmark! The U. S. Greeting Card Association (yes, there really is one) estimates that about a billion Valentine cards will be sent out this year. That's a billion pieces of pink and red heart-shaped manufactured tree bark, folks! This is second only to Christmas, by the way. And have you bought a card lately? They want me to pay $3.45 for someone else's thoughts and words to give to the most important person in my life? I mean, if I can't muster up an "I love you" or "You mean so much to me", then I'm in some real trouble over here. I told you I ain't buyin' in to it.

So here's what I came up with when my wife (then girlfriend) and I started going out and the "Corny Cupid Day" came around for the first time in our relationship. I stated to her that I didn't wish to choose just one day along with the rest of the country to declare my love for her; I 'd hope to show her in little ways throughout *every* day how I felt about her and ultimately how much she meant to me. (I know, I couldn't believe I came up with something this good either!) Anyway, she fell for it, I mean, believed me, and I've been off the hook every Valentine's Day since. That's right friend; no candy, no jewelry, no flowers, no cards. February 14 is just another day at our house.

But you know what? Just to be safe though, I might scribble on a piece of paper "You're the first, you're the last, you're my everything" and leave it on her pillow tonight.

THE BEAN BAG

That time is here. It can't be avoided any longer. I am going to finish off the basement.

I must admit that I'm going to miss that dank hollow cemented room with great acoustics. Stuff I haven't used in years piled on top of each other feeding off of dustbunnies. Those things that I just couldn't part with or put in a yard sale---they all got shoved over in the corner on top of some rusty metal shelf, making the perfect right angle for a spider web.

But it's time to ship those things to the garage or attic so my kids one day will have to take them to the dump. And it's time to transform this cave into a warm and friendly rec room. All this sounds good on paper and looks quick and easy on HGTV, but my stomach starts knotting up at the thought. The thought of moving all this stuff, studded walls, carrying cumbersome sheets of drywall down steps, mud, tape, sanding, painting, flooring, and then finding a new corner for all that stuff to live in.

But I got excited for the first time the other day when I realized what grand, glorious and forgotten piece of furniture will serve as the centerpiece for the new area: a bean bag. That's right, how great is a bean bag! Growing up, my brother and I got in some pretty good fights over who'd get to sit in the bean bag.

In college, I took a class titled "History of Furniture." So basically this prepared me so that I now can fake my way through a conversation about the early Etruscan curule chairs up to a Federal style tea-top table. Okay, so maybe these two things are all I remember---no wait, I also learned that Queen Anne had no direct bearing on the furniture named for her and Chippendale is not just a dancer wearing a bowtie.

Nonetheless, my point is that I don't recall the fabulous and brilliant design of the bean bag chair filling the pages of any of my furniture textbooks. And by fabulous and brilliant, I submit that this "low-seater" has it all. The chair, filled with its tiny Styrofoam beans, conforms to your contour for substantial support of the lumbar. Need a cupholder? Just choose any place on the floor within a comfortable arm-reach distance. No leaning down, causing flaring back pain, to play with your cat or dog---you're conveniently at ground level. Runaway popcorn kernels and Pop-Tart crumbs? Just a quick twirl in the air and your bean bag is crumb free. And that grape juice spill? Just wipe it off with a Clorox wipe. Bean bags come in different sizes, any color and can even be monogrammed so you and your brother can civilly have your own.

So I feel that any furniture savvy that I possess (which obviously ain't much!) will be satisfied once the ever classic bean bag chair is enshrined to its rightful and respectful place inside the deserving and preserving walls of the Smithsonian. Right in between Arthur Fonzarelli's leather jacket and Dorothy's ruby slippers.

THIS IS, UNDOUBTEDLY, BY FAR, THE BEST STORY YOU WILL EVER READ

Okay, let me just go ahead and warn you right now that, unless you have unusually and extremely low expectations or you've absolutely never read any piece of written word ever written, then the title of this article may be a bit misleading. Now, any good English teacher (or is it *well* English teacher? I never can remember), will emphasize that any article, poem, essay or story needs to have an "attention getter." And that first "attention getter" that lures a reader to its content is the title. So if you've made it this far, then I'm batting a thousand!

But this over-dramatized attention-getting title theory doesn't just apply to writing; people use this to begin conversations in which they emphatically want to make a point. I get a kick out of those who subscribe to this because it's almost like they have to lead with an incredibly strong statement because, for some reason, they believe that I'm not going to take seriously what they're about to tell me. Let me explain.

The other day I was driving back home and it was raining. It was raining hard. Honestly, really hard. My wipers were struggling to keep the windshield visible. But nonetheless, it lasted for about eight minutes, the grass got muddy, the streets were puddled and all was dry again the next morning. I talked to a friend of mine after the fleeting storm, and the first thing he said was, "I have never in my entire life seen it rain that hard!" Really? Ever? In your *entire* life? You remember Hugo in '89? Andrew in '92? They were pretty hard rains. Might want to rethink that statement.

Another one is the temperature when the mercury slid past the 100 mark. Another friend said to me, "In all my days, I can't honestly remember when I've ever been as hot as I was today!" Wow! Honestly? In all your days? Do you happen to remember last August? Or the one before that? They were in the 100s, too. But don't get me wrong; I'm impressed.

Or how about this one? Another friend went to a concert. I asked him how it was and he proceeded with this, "I kid you not, I heard the best song I've ever heard and probably will ever hear!" Whoa! He just kidded me not! And then made the bold prediction that no other piece of music will ever match it. Apparently he's never heard "Amazing Grace" or "The Star-Spangled Banner."

Now don't get me wrong, I completely understand that we all, even me, use these over-the-top statements. It's how we're programmed. We get excited about something and immediately feel the need to embellish it before we ever get to telling what it is we're excited about. What is that about us? Maybe I don't understand *why* we do it; I just know that we *do* do it. We're just like a dog; before you ever give him his treat, he's about wagged himself senseless over the anticipation of it.

Anyway, I'm pretty sure that I don't have a point or even much of a reason for bringing any of this up, other than the fact that I find it highly entertaining when I hear somebody start a story like this. And I bet you before the day is done, you'll hear somebody lead off with one of these big-time attention getters. You never know, it might even be me!

BIGGEST GAME OF THE YEAR

I just finished watching the biggest game of the year! Oh no, it wasn't the World Series or the Stanley Cup or even the Super Bowl---it was a whole lot better than those games. Oh, don't get me wrong, I love watching baseball, hockey, football and even keep up weekly with the point standings in NASCAR. But the training, physical and mental toughness, guts and skill of these amazing athletes don't even compare to the players in the game I just finished watching!

One of the best parts about this game is that it's practically on every channel. Heck, sometimes I can't get away from it! And the pregame hype? Whew! It's been going on for months! Oh yeah, I've seen where "experts" have written books about it and the best strategy on how to win it. Every long-winded fella with a radio talk show is usually talking to some of the past players and racers, and they're all sharing how their game plan worked better than their opponents'.

Now if you like rough sports, which most sports are, you gotta love this game! Football's got tackling, Hockey's got checking, Basketball's got fouling and Boxing's got punching, but these guys get downright ruthless. At least you *can't* hit below the belt in Boxing! And the girls are the worst! Oh, it's not just for guys. The ironic part is that girls couldn't even have anything to do with this game for a long time, but back in the 20's they started getting involved and now some of them are atop the leaderboard.

To go along with suckerpunches, this sport has got lying, stealing, cheating, backstabbing, bribing and just like any sport, money buys you the best players. And everybody gets into it. Big time! My neighbor hangs out his favorite team flag according to the season, but my whole street had their yards all littered up with who they were pulling for this year.

Here's one of the main things about this game that just doesn't make sense to me though: the commentators. I know everybody's got something to say about anything; I'm not talking about that. I'm talking about the fact that they can't wait until it's over. Not that they *can't* wait, they *don't* wait! Every single one of them is jumping in their seats raising their hands blurting out, "Oh me, oh me, I know first! I said the winner first!" Shut up and let the fat lady sing! I don't remember Howard Cosell announcing the victor in the middle of the third quarter of a tight football game on Monday night! Dan Bonner has never shouted out the winner of a NCAA March Madness basketball game with 8 minutes left in the second half! So what gives *these* commentators the right to make such outrageous claims before the final buzzer sounds? In fact, back in 2000, these "experts of the game" tried to predict the results and helped a pretty great deal in messing up the outcome and we didn't know for sure who won until about a month and half after the game was over!

The biggest difference in this game and every other game is that the race is competed and finished before anything is ever done. At the end of any sport, one can look back and see what was done or not done which directly resulted in the final outcome. Not in this race. Everybody's betting on the come. The anticipation. The race seems to be over but in reality, the announcer just said, "Gentlemen, start your engines."

I'd love to talk some more about this great event, but remaining true to the spirit of a real fanatic, I've got to go watch some postgame commentary. I think they're getting ready to project the winners for next year's elections!

CAR UN-ALARMS

Don't you just hate it when a really good idea is used so much that people don't pay attention to it anymore? No I'm not talking about yellow stoplights, but rather car alarms.

To catch you up, there is a lot of buzz going on about car alarms. By Googling those two words, over 26 million results show up. A lot of these are sites selling the alarms, a lot are sites showing you how to install them and how they work, and a lot of them are articles in opposition to the noise they produce and wanting to ban their existence for a more peaceful and not so distracting world. I understand most of these 26 million results and their reasons, but what I find interesting is that the original intent and purpose for the invention of the car alarm is not heeded by the passerby-er anymore because it is more annoying than alarming.

Recently I was standing on the sidewalk downtown talking with a couple of friends. A half block away, a horn started blaring and lights went flashing. None of the three of us ever turned our attention to the distraction that was trying desperately to interrupt our conversation. After about 10 seconds, one of us stopped in mid-sentence and we all turned to look up the street in irritation. "Will somebody shut that stupid thing up?" We all three just waited and watched while some guy hurriedly tried to get in the driver's side. Finally, after fumbling with different keys, he got in, started it up, silenced the temporary noise pollution and sped off.

Was this man the rightful owner? I have no idea. Whoever he was, I was championing him to just relieve the noisy situation at hand. And I'm sure if he would have pulled out a hammer and bashed through the window, I would have said to myself, "he must have lost his keys. Glad that alarm stopped though."

There's a statistic out there that states a car is stolen every 20 seconds in the United States. No wonder---it's because of noisy car alarms! To really deter a car thief, instead of a horn blasting out, automakers should design a locked car-door handle that oozes a molasses and tar mixture when tampered with. If I saw some guy running through a parking lot with black sticky hands, I'd chime right in with a hearty "Stop thief!"

My truck came with a factory installed alarm. I have accidentally set it off twice. I went in to panic mode. I started pressing buttons on my key-thingy, kicked a running board, frantically opened the door, desperately searching for the correct key to stick into the ignition, all the while applying the brake. In the midst of the action, I think I even popped the hood and reset my odometer. I finally got it turned off. With beads of sweat starting to form, I began checking out my surroundings with embarrassment. And then I had a sudden pang of realization: nobody was paying attention to me because nobody pays attention to loud annoying car alarms anymore!

So anyway, once upon a time, there was this shepherd boy who cried, "Wolf!"

VEHICULAR ENTERTAINMENT

Delaware plates were always the hardest ones to find. Pennsylvania cars seemed to be everywhere. And Indiana tags were the tricky ones because there were various kinds with varying colors and designs; had to be careful not to count those twice. Basically, what I'm trying to say here is that I was champ at finding the most cars from different states on interstate en route to the family vacation destination every summer. At the risk of bragging, I couldn't be beat!

I also held a few titles at Car Bingo, too. Start with the letter A, find some thing out the window beginning with that letter, the first one to announce their find is awarded a point, and move through the alphabet. Q and X were always a challenge, but I'd convince the other players every time that that robin flying overhead was really a quail and that car we just passed had an X-ray machine in the backseat.

Another version of that game was to start with A and find that letter on a road sign. I guess this was considered the Car Bingo 2.0 version.

Twenty Questions is a classic standby. I loved this one! Nothing will kill 100 miles quicker than this game. And the more obscure the person, place or thing, the better. The last time I played this game with the kids in the car, my "thing" they had to guess was Jimmy Wetzel's horse. Yeah, me neither. I have no idea who Jimmy Wetzel is or that he even had a horse. That was the last time they asked me to play!

So I was reminded of these classic car games this past vacation trip when, 27 miles in to the trip, I started to hear the dreaded "are we there yet?" from the backseat. Relying heavily on today's technology and automobile conveniences, I usually (and quickly) put in *Megamind* or *Toy Story* and sweet silence is victorious for the next two hours. Heck, sometimes, they're already arguing over what the on-road feature presentation is going to be even before we reach the mailbox! These are the times when I reach way down deep in the console to retrieve that single plastic artifact of my childhood time machine. With an over-confident wink and nod to my wife, I hand a cassette tape to the little riders in the back. Then I ask, "What do y'all think this is?" Some good entertainment for the next 50 miles.

When they finally give up, we move on to some AlphaBingo and License Plate I Spy. I'm telling you though, I'm still the champ!

So let's end with this: I'm thinking of a place. Go...

EXTERNAL SEASONAL ILLUMINATION

Let me just say two things once and for all: the Christmas lights have gotten way out of hand and I love it!

Every year it seems that Christmas comes earlier and earlier. At this rate, in the year 2020, Christmas will be celebrated 2 weeks before Halloween! But seriously, I know there are those of you who defiantly stand up for Thanksgiving and make sure that Santa doesn't tramp right over this holiday, getting ready for the crazy Black Friday early bird doorbustin' sales. I applaud you folks. In fact, I'm pretty sure I'm even on your team.

But I have to admit, I love me some Christmas and the sooner the better. I don't mean any disrespect to Thanksgiving---just the little kid in me can't wait for the snow and listen to the music and see all the lights. And the lights is what it's all about for me at Christmas.

I can remember from the early annals of my little tyke days, coming home from school and bee-lining into the living room where our glorious tree would stand, waiting to be lit up. I'd lie on the floor, daydream, pretend, talk to myself, take a nap---whatever, just as long as I could be by the tree. I'd scarf down dinner so I could go back and play by the tree. I'd even enjoy doing my homework by the tree!

To clear up any false implications here, I *didn't* necessarily enjoy putting the lights on the tree or even decorating it. I was just into reaping the fruits of someone else's labor. (Okay, my mom's labor!) It's a lot like pictures: I don't like taking them but I love looking at them. Same

43

with trees. Don't care much for decorating but love looking at them. Some might think this a somewhat unfair and one-sided attitude and approach. To you I must say, "You are completely correct."

So now you understand why I look forward to riding around, appreciating to the utmost, the display of external seasonal illumination in all its glorious grandeur. Throw in some kids in the backseat bursting with excitement hollering, "Oh look, another one!" and you've got what one songsmith called *the most wonderful time of the year*.

I'm not sure if it's the Christmas season that makes the lights or if it's the lights that make the season---don't think it matters. From oversized yard balloons to outlining rooftops, blanketing bushes, motorized reindeer to the simple and classic candles in the windows, no other holiday has embraced the lights like Christmas. Just another example of how special and exclusive this time of the year is.

So here's my point: if you don't have any lights up, put a candle in the window and see if the spirit of the season doesn't swell inside of you a little bit. And if your yard is saturated with decorations to a degree that would even make Clark Griswold shed a tear, thank you for "brightening" up the season for all of us. And next year see if you can't fit in a few more because the more the better and I love it!

FINDING THE NEEDLE

The smallest things can trigger the biggest memories.

I subscribe to a magazine called *Country*. It's a wonderful read with wholesome stories, homespun humor, delicious recipes, and pictures of America's countryside so breathtaking you'd think they were plucked from God's own wallet. But all of this is not why I get the magazine. In every issue, there is a needle that is hidden somewhere deep in one of the photographs in the pages. Yes, playing off the phrase "trying to find a needle in a haystack" idea. Just an extra little piece of fun for the readers to try and find.

Whenever I would go over and visit with my grandmother, she'd always have four materials she'd keep by her chair to read. The hometown paper, her Seek and Find puzzle book, *The Farmer's Almanac*, and *Country* magazine. She didn't need the TV Guide because she knew that Andy Griffith came on at 5:00 and "Wheel of Fortune", (or as she called it, Spin the Wheel) was on at 7:30. I always preferred crosswords over the seek-and-finds so I passed by that book. I didn't have a garden or needed to know the moon phases, so I never found much use for the Almanac. And I'd already read the paper.

So one day, she threw her *Country* magazine in my lap and said, "Here, help me find that dern needle." I didn't know what she was talking about so she explained to me the hunt. We looked through that magazine for 20 minutes together and finally found that dern needle. Like Columbus finally spotting land, we both sat back and breathed a sigh of victory.

The next week, luckily as time would have it, another issue showed up and the search was on. We found this one in the top left corner picture on page 29 just inside 17 minutes. We were getting better. This became our little game and with our two eagle eyes honed in, we couldn't be beat. Sometimes she'd find the needle before I got there and she'd say, "It's pretty tricky this time. Better look close." And sometimes she'd read her Almanac till I made it over so we could find it together.

Just like hearing the first few notes of a song can immediately take you back to a sweet place surrounded by long lost friends, or seeing a movie come on TBS or TCM can whisk you back to a high school date, seeing this magazine can drop me into that plaid sofa inside Grandma's overly warm living room with "Spin the Wheel" on in the background. I don't have any plans of ever letting my subscription run out.

Grandma changed her address eternally in 2004 and all these beautiful landscapes I enjoy in the magazine's photographs, she now gets to see in person whenever she wants. She shared wonderful stories, matured wisdom, and chocolate chip cookies with me. And still today, I can't really decide which one of these I enjoyed the most. But every time I pull that *Country* magazine out of the mailbox, I smile to myself and say under my breath, "Alright Grandma, let's go find that dern needle."

LIGHTS OUT

I'm sure most of us experienced the Great Blackout of 2012. The wind blew, ACs shut down, and a bunch of D-sized batteries were replaced in a rarely used Mag-Lite in the kitchen drawer.

How quickly we realized how dependent we are on the flip of a switch and a cool refrigerator waiting to be opened. No tv. No internet. No phone charger. And no nightlight in the bathroom. I can't tell if toothpaste is on my toothbrush! The small things in life we just don't realize.

So we lit candles, played cards and fondly reminisced about how wonderful it was living in the 21st century just a few days ago. Sitting in the dim glow of four candles and an eerily quiet house, I felt like Charles Ingalls was going to tap me on the shoulder and whisper, "It ain't easy, is it?"

But once my frustration of these modern conveniences being robbed subsided, I refocused. Don't get me wrong; I love technology. And am usually about ten feet away from a smartphone, iPad, or a laptop. But my newfound theory is that maybe these things are distractions to the core of what we are truly about. It gave this fast paced schedule a respite and a discovery of what's important in life.

Don't want to get all deep here, but let me put it this way. Some really smart men in the past had ample time to think and reflect and write and come up with some really brilliant ideas for us. And yes, you guessed it, most of these ideas were produced out of the supportive quiet and simple candle glow. I'm starting to think that TJ wouldn't have come up with our Declaration sitting in the AC in front of the boob tube. Or Martin Luther could have reformed the church listening to his iPod in a drive-thru. Or Ben Franklin would have been able to think up those witticisms and inventions while perusing Facebook watching *Hell's Kitchen*.

When the lights went out, our house grumbled at the sticky heat and we pretty much all stayed in one room. Especially at night...nothing spookier than those giant awkward shadows casted by a flashlight. The shadows scare me more than the dark! So for three nights there was a closeness and togetherness in one room that we hadn't experienced before. We hadn't been forced to. And it was nice. Just knowing we were all there if anyone needed anything in this different and unusual situation.

And when the lights came on, within minutes, one was in her room on her DS, another was watching tv, I went to my office to check emails, and my wife was in the laundry room. Once the house got cool, I thought about throwing the breaker so we could all meet up again in one room. No need to throw a breaker, but there's nothing wrong with taking a break from these wonderful modern conveniences now and then to help re-establish the fundamental good in what makes a family a family.

And I saw where that attitude spread rapidly throughout the community. A sense of togetherness and "let me know if you need any help" being offered at every tree that was down or deep freeze that was slowly warming up.

Personally, I believe out of every challenge comes a reward. I'm the first to admit that I missed my microwave and nightstand lamp. But it gave me time to refocus. Time to realize. Time to connect. Time to be thankful. And ultimately be reminded of Who is in control and who is not.

LYRICAL CONFUSION

Voltaire was once quoted, "Anything that is too stupid to be spoken is sung." As a songwriter and singer, I strongly disagree. I choose to believe that Voltaire simply didn't have rhythm and therefore to compensate for his melodic shortcomings, he spouted this off one day. Yeah, that's what I'm saying happened.

Nonetheless, I've never felt that the writer or singer is stupid, but the listeners to some songs could qualify. Okay, let's be fair, stupid is a bit harsh and not a pretty word, and I certainly don't believe that people who listen to music are stupid. So let's just say some of the following samples are examples of simply being mistaken. We've all been guilty of wanting to belt out a song in the shower or car and had to stop because we only knew the first two lines. Maybe the only thing worse than not knowing the words is singing the wrong ones. One time on stage, I forgot the words to the entire second verse. Went completely blank. I made the whole verse up. It didn't make any sense, but lines 2 and 4 rhymed and I smiled pretty. Epic fail averted.

Here are a few songs I've found myself singing along to, a bit incorrectly and, if you're Voltaire, stupidly, shall we say.

I have brown eyes and have always liked donuts. So you can imagine how happy I was when I heard Crystal Gayle's "Don't It Make My Brown Eyes Blue" because I thought she was saying "Donuts make my brown eyes blue." And then I heard Kenny Rogers sing about a man sitting at the bar desperately pleading with his wife, "You picked a fine time to leave me Lucille, with four hungry children and a crop in the field." However, I thought that man said, "with four *hundred* children and a *cop* in the field." The Duggars ain't no match for this dude!

And I never could understand why Patti LaBelle was so excited about her new kicks in her hit song, "I've Got a New Pair of Shoes." What? Oh, it's "I've Got a New Attitude." But the first lines are "Runnin' hot, runnin' cold, I was runnin' into overload." She's doing a lot of runnin'. Needs some shoes, right?

I thought Sir Paul was totally smoking his shorts in the Beatles classic "Michelle." "Michelle, my belle, some day monkey won't play piano song." I'm sorry, what? Maybe my French is a little rusty.

How about Johnny Cash's hit reminiscing about the family singing in the house when "Daddy sang bass, momma sang tenor." And before me and little brother joining right in there, I thought "Daddy sang bass and momma made dinner."

And one of my favorite easy rock 70s ballad is the Eagles' "Desperado." It has some great lines in it and I can remember every time Don Henley got to the line, "you've been out riding fences, for so long now..." I always sang along with him, "you've been outright offensive, for so long now..." There's a romantic thought that will simply endear your loved one forevermore.

And then there's that one rap song...who I am kidding? I can't understand anything they're saying!

OLYMPIC BACKYARD GAMES

U-S-A! U-S-A! These are the chants going on inside every American home as we watch and root our country to victory and ultimate medal.

Other than the fact than it's all about sports, the thing I love most about the Olympics is that I get excited about watching certain sports that I hardly have ever seen before and even more so, have no idea how to score them or know what the overall goal and object of that sport is. I'm rooting for something when sometimes I don't even know what I'm rooting for. I'll see some 90 pound girl jump off a diving board and complete a double knotted turnbuckle twist with a cherry on top and gracefully enter the water with barely a splash, and then at the bottom of the tv screen, it reads .96458. What does that mean?! Is it good or bad? Can we just have a "thumbs up" and "thumbs down" rating system? The novice Olympian fan is struggling over here!

So then I thought that maybe, just maybe, they could merge and introduce a few minor additions to these sports so that we could understand them a little better. Possibly include some of the games that we grew up playing in our backyards so we could understand the skill involved and the rules at hand.

Such as...instead of Water Polo, how about Marco Water Polo. One country's athlete is blindfolded shouting "Marco!" while another country's athlete responds back "Polo!" and dives under the water to another location in the pool. Sure, they can still throw the ball if they want to...if the blindfolded guy just happens to get it in the net, his team gets a point.

I'd like to see breakdancing become part of the pommel horse. Sound crazy? Aw c'mon, they're practically doing it already on that two-handled stationary bull. Just throw an Alfonso breakboard on top of there, a little Herbie Hancock music in the background, and an occasional windmill and headspin, and see if the ratings for this event won't fly through the roof.

I know soccer is the new football, or actually and technically, it's the old football, well actually it's a ball kicked with a foot but we call it something different...moving on. What about taking soccer and incorporating some elements of Kick the Can? You see where I'm going with this. I'd like to see Landon Donovan and David Beckham try this new fangled sport on for size. And the product placement is endless. Coke can, Pepsi can, Starbucks tumbler. Big bucks, I tell ya. Money.

Or how about merging Horseshoes and Ghost in the Graveyard? Okay, never mind. Bad idea.

How about a couple of Slip-n-Slides meandering down a British knoll? And where's the Olympic skill with this, you ask? *Synchronized* Slip-n-Slide. That's right. You heard me.

And for the Grand Finale. Two man Big Wheel relay. Take eight of your best horse jockeys, put them on a tandem big wheel and rubbing is racing! Need I say more? I submit I do not.

So, it is entirely possible, I realize, that the esteemed Olympic Committee may not heed these suggestions. No worries, I am and will always continue to chant red, white, and blue for gold, silver, and bronze. U-S-A! U-S-A!

SPELLING B

Surfing channels, I recently passed by and watched some of the National Spelling Bee. Wow! If you ever want to feel stupid, just watch about four minutes of this. I was humbled and impressed at the entire competition. Kids from 10 to 14 years old were spelling words that I not only didn't know how to spell or know what they meant, I didn't even know these words existed in our language. As a writer and self-proclaimed logophile (good word, eh? Look it up!), I'm always intrigued by unusual and interesting words that we all have access to but sometimes rarely know or use. It's always good to have a few of these words in your back pocket to drop in a conversation, business lunch, or a job interview to impress others. It's all about making people believe you're smarter than you really are! Perception is everything.

Computers and smartphones come equipped with the application to auto-correct words that we misspell or even attempt to spell. A lot of times, the computer or phone will offer the word it thinks you are trying to type even before you've typed the entire word. And it's usually right. Now that's scary!

But here's an encouraging exercise that reinforces the "innate smarts" that the Good Lord planted in our heads. Let me explain with this simple test and example.

Unisg the icndeblire pweor of the hmuan mnid, aocdcrnig to rseecrah at Cmabrigde Uinervtisy, it dseno't mttaer in waht oderr the lterets in a wrod are, the olny irpoamtnt tihng is taht the frsit and lsat ltteer be in the rhgit pclae. The rset can be a taotl mses and you can sitll raed it whoutit a pboerlm. Tihs is bucseae the huamn mnid deos not raed ervey ltteer by istlef, but the wrod as a wlohe.

I know. It's pretty amazing. And it seems that we still have the smartest computer yet to be ever manufactured: the brain. This doesn't mean that we can get lazy and who cares about spelling? That attitude won't get you a smiley-faced "Good Job" sticker on your senior thesis. But it does mean that our brains can fill in the gaps and rearrange what is intended to be completely understood for the overall good. See, why can't my wife understand what I meant to say instead of what I really said? It certainly couldn't have been my fault...

Speaking of spelling, I'll share my personal experience. In the fifth grade, I was honored to have made it to the finals of the Scripps Howard Spelling Bee in my elementary school. A stage full of nervous kids waiting on that pronunciation of a word they probably have heard but never needed to spell. Armed with sweaty palms, a collared shirt, and a stomach full of butterflies building a nest the size of Gibraltar, I approached that cheap microphone, complete with the inevitable feedback. I waited for my word. *Badminton.* Enter long awkward silence. "Could you use it in a sentence, please?" Uh oh. The packed cafeteria was thinking the same thing I was. *He's stalling because he doesn't know how to spell it. You only ask that question if you're not initially confident.*

I knew what badminton was. I just played it yesterday in P.E. for Pete's sake!

"Origin, please?" Like this is going to somehow magically reveal the correct spelling. *Oh, he really isn't sure!* My mind was racing. It starts with a B, right? So I began to blurt out. B-A-D-M-I. Then another long awkward pause. Then a quick T-T-E-N. The buzzer stung my ears worse than that stupid feedback from the microphone. The announcer correctly spelled it for me and as I was exiting the stage, I felt the color come back in my face and those butterflies flew away. Surprisingly, I wasn't upset; the relief thankfully overpowered the nervousness.

Watching those kids on TV the other night, a few of those butterflies flew back in my stomach for them. I was glad I wasn't being asked to spell those words and was reassured in the intelligence of our youth today. And just for the record, I'll never misspell badminton. Never.

THE EARTH IS FLAT

One of the great debates throughout philosophical and scientific history is whether the Earth is flat. Living in the 21st century, thanks to modern technology, some floating satellites and Google Earth snapshots, it's easy to know and accept that we live on a big ol' spinning ball. So yes, the score to date is Pythagoras 1, Copernicus 0. Now I'm the first to tell you that when it comes to science, I'm not the best pickle in the barrel. And I've got the transcripts to prove it! So I'll leave the scientific proof of the Earth being round to NASA and all those with an eighth grade understanding on the subject. I do understand that you can sail around the world and not fall off. And I've seen that round shadow with no right angles casted by the Earth during an eclipse. What I'm interested in is the philosophical understanding of whether the Earth is flat.

And I submit, without a doubt, that it is. The world we know, is flat. My backyard. The street I drive on. The counter in my kitchen. The neck on my guitar. The cookie sheet in my cabinet. We are surrounded by flatness. And I'm a believer that we are given all these things in their raw natural state of being flat to make them fruitful and exciting and alive.

It's up to the gardener to plant flowers and shrubs and vegetables in that flat ground in my backyard to make it grow. It's up to the cook to use a plain flat counter to use bowls and pans and ingredients to make the food which helps us all become round. It's also up to that cook to fill that flat cookie sheet with flour, sugar and butter to help make us all even rounder. It's up to the gardener and it's up to the cook.

Every time new strings are put on a guitar, those strings, musically and tonality speaking, are flat. They are below the pitch. They need to be stretched and pulled and bent to bring them up to the note to make it pleasing to the ear. And once all of them are pulled to pitch, it's up to the player to pluck and slide this six-string army into the song that will uplift the flattest of moods and make the wariest and chariest dance with joy. It's up to the musician.

Take a good book, for example. Just black words on a white page. Flat as can be. It's up to the writer to make those words jump off the page and rest eternally in the imagination of the reader to convey the idea of reality. Those words, if simply told, are lifeless. Meaningless. And flat. But if those words are shown, the reader will live thankfully inside the story full of color with sights, sounds and smells included, in which these words have revealed and fulfilled to their utmost. It's up to the writer.

And speaking of good books, the Bible is the ultimate example of living in a flat world. Don't get offended yet, hear me out. Chocked full of stories after parables after lessons...divinely written and humanly read. But still, in its rawest form, the words lay flat on the page which lays flat between the cover which lays flat on the shelf. So it is up to the reader and understander to "unflatten" this book and its words and put these stories, parables, and lessons in to action. Bring them to life. Make them shine. Be inspired and show to the world what these words tell. Read them. Act on them. Cast your own round shadow from the light you are emitting from them. It's up to the believer.

Scientifically speaking, the world is round. Philosophically speaking, it's flatter than Mrs. Rowe's pancakes. It's up to us.

STATISTICS

Statistics. Better known as stats. Sounds better, not so stuffy and has a nice quick punch to it. And people can throw it around a lot easier. And oh boy, do people love to throw them around. And I guess the reason for that is because there is a stat for absolutely anything that has ever happened. In fact, there are just as many stats for the same number of everything that has *never* happened. A stat can be created out of anything. How many people read this column. How many people didn't read it. How many read it standing up. How many didn't read it while scrambling an egg before changing their oil. How many thought about reading it but decided to change their egg and scrambled their oil. Do I really need to explain further? Please say no! Like I said, there's a stat for everything.

And sports lovers are the biggest stat hogs on Earth. I was listening to the playoffs in the car the other night with a friend and it seemed as if every batter that stepped in the box, the commentator had a litany of numbers, comprising RBIs, HRs, SOs, BBs, ABs against lefties, BA in this stadium, Slugging Percentage with two strikes, and on and on. It was bit humorous listening to the man with the microphone fill up space with these impressive numbers. So my friend says to me, "Does anybody really pay attention to all these stats?" For some reason I felt compelled to rise to the defense of the "stat hungry" folks and responded, "Championships are built on this stuff!"

After reading the look on his face, I explained further. "The Pitching Coach is briefing the pitcher before each inning as to where to and not to pitch his first three batters up, based on the history of their meetings over the last season. Every batter has his weakness in the box and it's the pitcher's job to find it." As if on cue, Ryan Flaherty, from the Orioles, sent one airmail to the cheap seats. "See, somebody for the Yankees didn't pay attention to the stats on Ryan." And then the commentator chimed in, "For you stat lovers out there, Flaherty becomes the first player from the state of Maine to hit a home run in a post season game." So I guess some stats are important and others ain't so much.

Other than watching the playoffs and reruns of *Alf,* somebody said something about an election fixing to happen. Okay, maybe sports fans aren't the worst when it comes to stats; these political junkies and analyst groups spend lots of time and way too much money on the statistics of people who voted when, where and why. The one stat they keep ignoring is that 100% of America just wants the truth. If they spent that time and money on finding that candidate, we'd have us something then. And how can I believe in these stats and polls when nobody's ever asked me? It can't be accurate in my eyes until I chime in, right?

So one presidential stat I keep hearing is that Ohio has sided with every winning president since 1944, except one (Nixon). That's why the candidates are trying to open as many buckeyes as they can. Sure, it seems to be a good indicator of how the votes will fall, but what about the other 56...excuse me, 49 states? Do they not matter? With this kind of thinking, just let Ohio cast their votes and we won't waste time with predictions and projections.

I do realize that there is some validity and value in statistics. We have to know the past before we step into the future and statistics help us make this step easier to take. I get it. But I also get this part: you either take that step or you don't. It's a 50% chance you will and 50% chance you won't. You either vote red or blue. Flaherty either hits that home run or he doesn't. And you either read this column or not. Well, actually, if you got this far, it's 100% chance you did!

EVERYONE'S AN EXPERT

When I was growing up, I used to sit in my room and play solitaire for hours on end. My dad would come in, sit on the edge of my bed, look over my shoulder, and always find a move I was missing. I'd thank him for his help but would ask him, "If two people play solitaire, it can't be called solitaire can it?" Pretty good question, ain't it? Anyway, I remember his response would always be, "Son, just remember, if you're ever stranded on a deserted island, pull out a deck of cards and start playing solitaire, 'cause undoubtedly someone will come along and show you a move you're missing."

Well, as I've gotten older, I've found that that strange and humorous logic can apply elsewhere in life. Wondering what I'm talking about? Well, just go plant you some grass. That's right, plant some grass.

Here's what I did exactly four weeks ago: I cleared some brush, threw some grass seed down on some plowed up dirt and put some fertilizer on top of this for good measure. To top it off, I covered it all with straw so the birds wouldn't eat my seeds. The days it didn't rain I watered it in the evenings. After four weeks, I'll admit, it's not as plush as the second cut at Sawgrass, but it's greener than that yellow straw and brown dirt a month ago.

And you wouldn't believe the unsolicited advice I've gotten from everybody and their brother on this grass growing matter:

"Your seed is spread too thin."

"You need to water more."

"You're watering too much."

"Your straw is choking the seed."

"Not enough shade."

"You need some Class A Quality Rate Turf Builder."

"Try pouring a mixture of vinegar and stale buttermilk over top it."

"You should've planted earlier in the spring."

"You need to plant late in the fall."

"I'd've put mulch down."

"The almanac says stagger your seed and fertilizer according to the third tidal moon phase."

So there you have it. I've yet to have one person say, "Hey, good job on your grass. It looks good." I've learned that everybody is an expert when it comes to telling you what you've done wrong. Just once I'd like for an "expert" to say, "I'm an expert and you've done everything right!"

My point is, is that there's only so much you can do when it comes to planting grass. You take what the good Lord gives you and leave the rest up to Him. Ain't that like life? You just do the best you can with what you've been given, and leave the rest up to the Big Man in the Sky. And you can believe me 'cause I'm an expert!

THE FIRST FAMILY BEACH VACATION

This summer I went on vacation. To the beach. With the family. And I mean the *whole* family. 7 days, 6 nights, 5 cars, 4 generations, 3 dogs, 2 three year-olds all in 1 house. The only thing missing was a wood-sided station wagon with a canoe on top and we would have been the poster family for every postcard rack up and down the Atlantic. With a suitcase packed with only swimming suits, t-shirts, suntan oil and an iPod, I beached myself silly! And I never imagined I'd go 36 hours without wearing any underwear! But then, you probably didn't need to know that.

Now I'd love to get right into some hilarious story that resulted from all the diverse complexities that collided with the idiosyncrasies from each individual family member. Believe me, I know this would make for a colorful and entertaining story. And I'd love to think that my family vacation could bring Chevy Chase out from wherever he is and they'd base the next *Griswold's Go to the Beach* movie on our experiences. And I'd love to use one of those witty one-liners about how we "put the fun in dysfunctional!" But much to my chagrin of a vacation full of family wackiness, I'm going to have to tell you the truth. So brace yourself, because most writers are trained to sensationalize, embellish and dramatize the pleasant and mundane just to pique a reader's interest. That's not the case with what I'm about to share with you. So here goes.

As I've already implied, the house was full of 11 people, all with different personalities, interests and schedules. In any book, a recipe for disaster. But not necessarily.

Each morning, the little ones would beat the rooster out of bed, ready to get their beach on! The rest of us would stagger out of our bedrooms, groggy-eyed and with a serious case of bed head, and would find ourselves sitting quietly on the top deck of the house with a cup of coffee. We weren't quiet because we were tired; it was because we were sitting there in some handmade wooden Adirondack chairs staring at the Sun making its way from behind a glistening and colorless ocean. The sight demanded reverence. I remember from ninth grade Earth Science that the Sun is 93 million miles from us and provides heat for the entire world, but I swear to you, I felt like I could reach right out and pet it and that it was making its glorious entrance just for me and no one else. So here we are still in our pajamas, each of us cradling a cup of coffee, the kids watching cartoons in the background, waves crashing intermittently to remind us how powerful and majestic the ocean really is and the Sun presiding over us all with its rays outstretched like arms giving the whole world a big bear hug. It was obvious this was going to be a good day!

The feel of the sand sliding smoothly between your toes is a feeling that I've never heard anybody complain about. It's just like somebody scratching your back; you never get tired of it and it always feels good. And then I found amazing how a $3 bucket full of plastic toys could sculpt a rather impressive sand castle complete with a moat, a tunnel for backdoor escapes and a customized seashell pit. And speaking of seashells, I know they're like pocket change to God, but it's like a million bucks to a three-year old who finds out that whatever she finds, she can take home.

I'm not sure how it's possible, but the Sun is never as hot or cruel at the beach as it is back home when I'm mowing or weed eating. When I'm at home, I do all I can to hurry up and get out of the heat. But at the beach, I hurry up to get out in it. And then I say, "Aw, this feels so nice." Maybe it's because my refreshment is within twenty feet; water for as far as I can see just begging me to come jump in a try to ride a wave. No matter how warm the water might be, it still initially takes my breath. And I'm never quite ready for that first wave to smack me in the swimming suit, shoot saltwater up my nose and leave me embarrassingly sitting on my backside while, all around me some foamy waters laughingly head back out to sea.

As for a schedule at the beach, to each his own and we'll see you for dinner at six. Dinnertime is probably my second favorite part of the vacation. And not just because it has to do with food. Everybody is all squeaky clean with their newly bronzed cheeks and red shoulders and khaki shorts and flip-flops. The guys of the troop would oversee the grill duties while the ladies would bake potatoes, casseroles or some dessert fluffed high with meringue. A blessing of thanks would be said and we'd all commence on our servings. All the while quizzing the little ones on what their favorite part of the beach was that day or what kind of sand monster they're going to make tomorrow. And I always noticed that we never had anything in particular to talk about, we just talked. And you know that's what families do. You don't have to have a reason or a purpose to say something. If something's on your mind, be it a story, a joke or a silly thought, just say it. 'Cause we're all here on vacation and we're family; that's what a family vacation is for.

And then after dinner and little people bedtimes, we'd all end up back out on that same deck where our day had so blessedly started. The Moon had assumed the prime seat in the sky and would share his reflections with us using the glassy surface of the ocean. Usually enjoying a second helping of dessert or a vanilla cigar, I felt like I owned the night. The Moon, the water, the breeze, the distant lights, and the thought of being surrounded by those who love you and make you feel good and happy. *This* is my favorite part.

So there it is. Our first family beach vacation. I warned you that it wasn't too exciting or full of colorful mishaps and family drama. Just multiply this day by seven and that was our vacation. Kind of boring? For some maybe. Kind of old-fashioned? I'm sure of it. Would I do it again? Can't wait.

THE DIFFERENCES BETWEEN MEN AND WOMEN

I hate I have to be the one to tell everybody this, but it's something you really need to know. Men and women are different. Seriously, we are not the same. And I know what you're thinking; *but Thomas Jefferson said that all of us were created equal and stuff.* I know, I had that Social Studies textbook book cover with that quote on it, too. I'm pretty sure that what he was meaning to mean is that we're all given the same opportunities. But actually being created equal? Sorry Mr. President, issue will have to be taken.

Now that John Gray fella a few years back tried to get this point across. Yes, you remember him! He's that guy who wrote the book and traveled with the seminars saying that *Men Are From Mars, Women Are From Venus.* His unaccredited background still has many wondering about the validity of his book and theories, but I can assure you that *I* know what I'm talking about. No, I don't have a Ph.D., probably just A.D.D. at best. No, I haven't taken any higher courses in relationships or gender difference studies. And no, I've never even talked to anyone certified in this area to enlighten me on why men and women are the way they are. But, however, my research is insistent and indefatigable to the utmost because I *am* a man and I have *observed* the idiosyncrasies of the woman. I confide in you, right here and now, that I am a self-proclaimed expert on the matter.

And now that I have clearly stated my credentials, here are the main differences between a man and a woman, categorized and classified for easier understanding. Oh and just a quick heads up on what you're about to read; if you are a member of the male or female gender, there is the slightest chance that you may be offended. But hopefully you'll be more enlightened and entertained and you'll forget that you might have been offended. Nonetheless, can't say I didn't warn you!

Fashion
Men will wear socks and pants multiple days in a row. If the clothes in question pass the "smell test", then we're good to go.
Women will change outfits thrice daily. Sometimes even more, I just like using the word thrice.

Financial
Men view gambling as another source of income. And when we lose, we only see that it's that much more we have to win.
For women, the word "sale" is like kryptonite. They immediately succumb to its power.

Sex Appeal
Men have been happy with every haircut we've ever received. You probably haven't noticed because we're wearing a ballcap.
Women have never been completely satisfied with the overpriced cut, color or style they've received. Y'all wanna borrow one of our ballcaps?

Home Décor
Women enjoy watching numerous home shows and reading magazines on how to decorate the Living Room just right.
Men don't even know we have this room in the house. We recognize 5 rooms: den, kitchen, bedroom, bathroom and garage.

Entertainment
Men can pick up in the middle of any Steven Seagal movie and be entertained.
Women can pick up in the middle of *Steel Magnolias* and still cry.

Relaxation
Women light a sugar cookie scented Yankee candle, take a hot bath and listen to Christopher Cross' "Sailing."
Men play 27 holes while puffing on stogies and munching on cool ranch Doritos and afterwards do not realize that we smell like a two-day old burrito dipped in onion teriyaki sauce.

Physical Attributes
Men are totally unaffected by their hormones.
*Woman can bear children.

Appreciation of American Pop Culture
Women watch "Dancing With the Stars" for the costumes.
Men watch "Dancing With the Stars" for the costumes. (These two may sound the same but I think we all know what I'm talking about here!)

Intelligence
Men know the difference between pliers and vice grips.
Women know the difference between the colors salmon, coral and melon.

So in conclusion, please do not, under any circumstances, try to sell anyone at anytime on the belief of the idealistic and political correct theory that men and women are somehow the same. Are we clear?

*This one's a biggie!

WEATHER FORECAST: WHO CARES?

"Boy, Thursday was cloudy."

"It's callin' for rain tomorrow."

"The sun's supposed to be out all day long."

Have you ever been caught saying one of these phrases? Don't feel bad if you have, because, in fact, most people have said them. A lot of people everyday talk about the weather. Mark Twain once said "Everybody talks about the weather, but nobody does anything about it." How true. That fella should've been a writer or something.

My wife is just eat up with the weather. Planting a garden and watering flowers and rain gauges and setting her mums inside in fear of frost; did I mention, she's just eat up with the weather? The first thing she does in the morning is turn the tv on channel 24. That's the Weather Channel. I still can't believe this. Weather has its own channel. Weather! It's not a person or thing, it's like an indescribable unknown event depending on the moon, tides and God's mood. And it has its own channel! That's as crazy and absurd as if History had its own channel! Wait a minute...

But back to my wife. She watches the forecast and the radar and the moving cloud cover map. She then switches over to the Soap Opera channel, then back to the Weather channel, then over to Oprah, then the weather, then some nights she watches that *Extreme Desperate Housemaker* show and then finally back to the weather.

Now I'm fully aware that there are lots and lots of people out there who are just like her when it comes to being eat up with the weather. And I'm fully aware that the weather has been mystifying and intriguing people since the beginning of time. But what mystifies and intrigues me is not the weather, but those who care this much about it. I don't mean to offend those who are, but seriously folks, who cares? Like that Twain fella said, can't nobody do anything about it. It doesn't do any good for us to complain about it. And we can't change it. In fact, the only time I even take notice of it, is on a beautiful day when I take a quick moment and thank the Big Man in the Sky for being in a good mood that day and giving us a pretty one. Now you farmers out there, of course you all have to keep an eye on the weather. But y'all also work from sun up to sun down; when do you have time to watch tv?

But the weathermen all over the world prove everyday that you can study and predict and forecast and dopplerize but you still are not going to come up with a surefire answer for what the Good Lord's going to do that day. You know, I'm pretty sure that being a weatherman is probably the best job in the world; you can be 100% wrong and still not lose your job. Don't we make fun of a palm reader for trying to predict the future, but give us a weatherman and we'll check in with him six times a day and plan our entire week around what he says.

Well, I'm going to get real basic here with my logical thinking and help everybody out. Here are a few things in the future to do when wondering about the weather:

If you're inside, look out a window.
If it's raining, go inside.
If it's snowing, wear mittens.
If it's cold, put on a coat.

If it's hot, wear shorts.
And if it's pretty, thank the Lord.

I hope these things will help out when worrying yourself silly about that weather. I just hope I haven't put those nice folks over at the Weather Channel place out of business. That Twain guy also said that "Climate is what we expect but weather is what we get." That's true, too! I'm telling you, that guy was smart.

INDEPENDENCE: A RISK WORTH TAKING

Independence. A pretty big word. And I'm pretty sure I learned the concept of it before I ever learned exactly what it meant or how to spell it. I started implementing the idea of independence somewhere around six months old when I wanted to hold my own bottle instead of letting anyone else hold it for me. And from hearing the stories that followed suggesting my "headstrong behavior" thereafter, it's safe to assume that I was six months going on eighteen years old. If I could have had my own apartment, paid taxes and worked a remote control, I'd've probably moved out of the house somewhere around the fall of 1975!

But this scenario is not unique to me; it's unique to all of us. All of us Americans, that is. Headstrong, particular, stubborn, determined, forthcoming---I don't care what you call it, it's the want and desire to be independent.

I remember sitting in the front row of my twelfth grade government class and our teacher pointing at us with her long painted red fingernail. She said, "Each one of you has an instinctive talent that can lift you higher than anyone else in the world. It's nothing you've asked for; you were just born with it. We're all Americans so therefore we're all risk-takers. It's a living part of who you are to take risks."

I wasn't completely sure what she was talking about that day but I get it now. The genetics of Americans. That red, white and blue fiber that we all share. All great people come from great stock. Take a look at our American "fathers." The forefathers of our nation. The architects of this country. George Washington, Thomas Paine, Thomas Jefferson, Benjamin Franklin, James Madison, John Adams, Patrick Henry---you know them all. They wore puffy shirts, powdered wigs, three-cornered hats and wrote their words of wisdom with quill pens. They may have looked like they lived in a different time but they were speaking about and for our times today. They were talking about independence. And they were taking huge risks for something better.

Every war and battle that we have shed American blood in has been invested on the side of helping declare independence. When you're independent you have the freedom to ultimately be yourself. To be strong. To be great. To be unlike those of whom you're instructed to follow and now be a leader for those to follow you.

All great ideas and people are only noticed once they are original, different or better. So I, along with you, tip my hat and salute those brave men and women and their families of revolutionary times for molding us into the original, different and better country that we are today. They took a risk to do what they believed to be true, right and good. They went against the grain and pursued the unpopular thought. They stood their ground and fought the hard wearisome fight. All to become independent. And I'm sure glad they did.

I'M A LEFTY, RIGHT?

The first big impressive word I learned at a rather young age was *ambidextrous.*

When walking to the plate at my first tee-ball practice, I hesitated for a moment not sure which batter's box to step in. *Am I right-handed or left-handed?* The only thing I knew for sure is that I was confused. My coach, with a concerned look on his face, ran over to me and asked, "What's wrong, buddy?"

"Which side do I hit from?"

He smiled and said, "Either one. Whatever feels the most comfortable."

I thought about it for a moment and innocently offered, "But both of them feel comfortable!"

"Aw, that's okay. You must be ambidextrous."

"Yeah, I must be." Yeah, what he said.

The end of this story is that I went home and told Mom and Dad that I loved tee-ball and I learned that I was amphibious. But this story was the beginning of a life-long search, never quite knowing if I'm a lefty or a righty. Here are my experiences to date.

I did find out that I bat and throw a baseball left-handed. This goes for basketball and football. The few times I've gone bowling, I nailed the gutter every time left-handed. However, I play tennis right-handed. I kick a soccer ball with either foot. I shoot pool right-handed, although, if finesse, strategy or a trick shot presents itself, I'll shoot from the left side. The first couple of years I went hunting, I always shot from the right shoulder. But then early one mornin' when the sun didn't shine, I heard some rustling to the right of me and that big oak tree was not going to let me "scope up" right-handed, so I went lefty. I didn't get anything that year but I did find out that I shoot just as good from the left side as I do from the right. But that still ain't saying much for fine marksmanship!

I eat with my right hand but I prefer my drink on the left side. I write with my right and wear my watch on my right wrist. I brush my teeth with my right, can effectively sweep out my garage holding the broom from either side, and when buying a new pair of shoes, I always try on the left shoe. When I cross the street, I'm never sure which way to look first so I only use crosswalks on One Way streets.

And here's the most complex: Golf. I drive and hit all my irons from the right side but come time to putt, I switch to the left side. For those of you keeping score at home, when I hit in a sand trap, I pick up the ball with my right hand and throw it on the green with my left. Okay, so I stretched it a little bit here, but nonetheless, if you're playing golf with me it can get pretty confusing!

I coached a 13-year old baseball team one year and one of the kids was in awe of my subtle ability to hit from both sides of the plate. "How cool is that that you can hit from either side!" Well, quite honestly, it's only cool if you can really pull it off. And I never could "really pull it off." Any base hits, home runs and first-place trophies that I have were all earned from the left side. So I regretfully shook my head to that impressed little leaguer and offered, "Hit from whichever side you can get on base with. People pay to see you get on base; not how you get there." About that time, another coach walked up behind me and said, "That's right. It's all about *what* you do; not *how* you do it."

And you now, as long as what you do is the right good thing, it really doesn't matter much how you do it. Although, I still wished I could've hit just one home run from the right side to brag to my grandkids about one day!

OLYMPIC FEVER

Okay, I admit it. I didn't get much done last week. It's not my fault, the Olympics were on! And I am hooked. Well, they say that's the first step: recognizing the problem, right?

I love the sports, the competition, the camaraderie among teammates, and the basic thrill of rooting for fellow Americans I've never met playing a game I don't even know the rules to.

There are a few things I've learned in the last week watching the Olympics. I've learned that I can't sit on the couch and eat an entire bag of Doritos and bounce back the next day like I did in college. I've learned that Coca-Cola and Visa have some pretty deep advertising pockets. (Well, I kinda knew that one already---got my credit card statement yesterday.) I am convinced that Michael Phelps has webbed feet and a dorsal fin. I learned that if you stay up till 3 a.m. and watch the 55k Freestyle Wrestling, there really is nothing else on. I'll never worry that a swimming cap will come in style. And I learned that I never get tired of hearing the National Anthem. What a beautiful song!

However, there are a few things that I don't know concerning these international games of feat. And lucky for you, I took notes along the way. So let me ask you:

1)   Why do you have to wear sunglasses in a 100 meter foot race at night?

2) Why do they have to shower immediately getting out of the pool?

3) How come foreign athletes are allowed to train in the U.S. but then compete under their own flag? I know it's legal, but it ain't right.

4) Why do the Chinese like Kobe Bryant more than the Americans?

5) Is that spotter under the uneven bars *really* going to catch that swinging gymnast if she falls?

6) How come I never saw the *Beijing 2008* logo printed anywhere in Chinese? Not upset about it, just curious.

7) When does Bob Costas sleep?

8) How come Indoor Volleyball has 6 players a side, but Beach Volleyball only has 2?

9) Do you have to dress like an astronaut in order to compete in fencing?

10) There's really a country named Togo?

11) Did I just watch badminton?

And finally:

When is the Elementary School P.E. classic game of Fishes & Whales going to be an Olympic sport? I promise you I will Platinum medal this when it happens!

In closing, just like the Olympics will do tonight, let me sign off with the very words of the Olympic Creed that make the promise of which these games have come to be about. This creed has been displayed proudly and appropriately on the scoreboard of every Olympic games since 1908. The Bishop of Pennsylvania, Ethlelbert Talbot, presented these words in a sermon for the athletes in London. "The most important thing in the Olympic Games is not to win but to take part, just as the most important thing in life is not the triumph, but the struggle. The essential thing is not to have conquered, but to have fought well."

Fellow American athletes, you did both. You fought well *and* you conquered.

FIVE MINUTES AIN'T WHAT IT USED TO BE

If you live in the middle of town and someone asked you how far it is to Wal-Mart, you'd probably say, "Aw, 'bout five minutes." And you'd be wrong. Don't feel bad, I'd say the same thing. And to be fair, if you went top legal speed at 3 a.m. and were lucky enough to hit every green light, five minutes *might* be possible. But in the middle of the day and without the help of the Traffic Gods smiling upon you, the quick and usual response of "just five minutes" is a bold face lie!

Now I feel confident in assuming that none of us are in the business of deliberately spouting off unthinking lies, so therefore, I must also assume that our understanding of real time is horribly skewed. Here's what I mean. It'll only take you five minutes.

I just finished redoing a room in the house. Don't even get me started on this whole undertaking but I will let you know how it ended. It was 5:15 and we were leaving the house at 5:30 for dinner. I decided to make maximum use of these few minutes before leaving: I was going to hang a picture in this room to finish it off. I grabbed a nail and a hammer for this simple task. I'm sorry, did someone say simple?

I tapped on the wall with my knuckle to find a stud. The nail went through that drywall like a machete through a beanbag. This stud-finding process always works for Bob Vila! Why not for me? Down the stairs to the garage to get one of them blue plastic anchors and a screw. Back upstairs. I then realized that the nail hole was not big enough for the anchor. *No big deal* I thought, *I'll just pound the anchor in with the hammer.* This really should've worked but all that happened was that plastic anchor just bent completely out of shape. Down the steps and back to the garage. As I was looking for an awl, or as I more accurately call it, "that-sharp-pointy-hole-pokey-thing," I noticed my family getting into the car. But because I have been blessed with the talent of a one-tracked mind and I finish what I start without proper consideration to others, back up the stairs I went.

After the hole was widened and drywall dust scattered on the carpet, the new anchor was in place as was the screw. But much to my carpentry chagrin, I now needed a screwdriver. Yes that orange-handled screwdriver in the garage! Did I mention I have a one-track mind? Insert expletive here. As I descended the stairs, I thought I heard a car motor. Must have been the angry thoughts forming into the heavy sighs. Once I retrieved the screwdriver, I noticed the garage was minus a car. Can't think about that now---I've got a picture to hang.

I topped the stairs, wiped the sweat from my brow and felt that first tinge of relief that this was going to finalize the makeover of this room that I thought was perfectly fine to begin with. The screwdriver kissed the head of the screw and I swear I could hear angels singing in praise that this process was coming to an end. But the screwdriver kept slipping off the screw head. The screw was not screwing. Why? Because it's impossible to turn a straight blade screw with a Phillips head screwdriver! Down the stairs. Insert different expletive here. I'd love to get Mr. Straight Blade and Mr. Phillips in a meeting and see if we can't work out some kind of truce. If not a merger, then maybe Mr. Phillips would consider a buy-out. It would certainly make my life a lot simpler.

I finally got the right screwdriver to put the screw in the anchor in the whole that the awl made for the picture to hang on the wall. After looking at the picture, I have to honestly admit that it really wasn't worth all this trouble. And after I got out of the shower (yes, I worked up enough sweat walking up and down those stairs that it warranted a shower!) the clock read 6:18. I missed dinner but did make it in time for dessert. And here are the lessons I learned: 1) I'm never hanging another picture. 2) When someone says "just five minutes," they're just trying to sucker you into an hour's worth of work that they don't want to do. 3) There are 17 steps in my house. 4) Wal-Mart is farther than you think but it doesn't matter 'cause you're still going anyway. 5) It probably took you longer than five minutes to read this column. See what I mean---it goes fast doesn't it?

I HAVE NO FRIENDS IN BIRMINGHAM

I recently flew. I've done it before and am sure will do it again. It's too convenient not to. I'm still amazed every time I glance down on top of a cloud that two brothers from North Carolina said this incredible feat could actually work. We've certainly come a long way in the aviation experience with the help of computers and a bunch of higher math formulas that make this bird fly straight. But it also amazes me the things we still need to work on to make the whole flying experience a bit more, well, just better.

Keep in mind, my ticket had already been bought and I'd flown through two airports and I'm in Birmingham at the check-in counter, homeward bound. I handed my pertinent info to the girl at the counter in hopes to receive my boarding pass.

"Use the kiush to check in."

"The what?"

"The kiush," as she pointed to the kiosk two feet in front of her.

"At first I thought this was some Jewish term I was supposed to know, but as it turned out, she was just phonetically challenged. The kiosk read INSERT CREDIT CARD HERE TO CONTINUE.

"Why do I need to use my credit card if I've already paid?" I felt this to be a logical question, but Miss Grammar thought otherwise.

"You ain't got to use your card. Just skip 'at screen and put your name in 'ere."

"Why can't you just do this, much like the other helpful ladies at the other ticket counters in other airports?"

"That's what the kiush is 'ere for."

"So what are *you* here for then?" Again, I deemed this another logical question worthy of an explanation.

Obviously irritated with my inquiries, she reluctantly abdicated her mighty throne from behind the counter to the kiosk, I mean kiush. After multiple attempts through multiple screens, my information had successfully escaped from the "flawless" computer system.

She went back to her counter and completed my boarding pass info just as the other helpful ladies had at the other ticket counters in other airports. "Hmmm...if you would have done this in the first place, you could be enjoying the memory of my company right now." I don't think she appreciated my point or sarcasm. I did thank her for her service and she just shrugged at me. So I told her it was pronounced *kiosk*, not *kiush*. She didn't thank me for my service.

I proceeded to the security officer who made sure my boarding pass and ID matched. I walked ten more feet and was instructed by another security officer to empty all my pockets completely, remove my shoes, and with arms extended, walk through the metal detector. I appreciate and applaud all these necessary security measures. I made it through without getting buzzed. This security officer then asked for my boarding pass.

"I don't have it. It's in my briefcase on the x-ray belt."

"Well, I need to see your pass, sir!"

"Then why did you just tell me to empty all my pockets and partially disrobe?" The logical questions were just flowing from me.

"Well, I can't let you pass through this gate if I don't see your boarding pass."

I took a long deep breath. "You can see my pass as soon as it comes out of the x-ray belt. But I struggle to understand that just a mere ten feet ago, a security officer who is within perfect earshot of our conversation, just checked my boarding pass and ID. How is it possible that this information that I just presented to him 30 seconds ago, could have somehow changed that would not allow me to participate in hopefully the final string of a litany of inconvenient activities I have endured since my arrival at this airport?"

He was not happy with my question as I was equally not satisfied with his attempt to answer. My question was not directed toward him or his responsibility to doing his job---I was wondering about the policy of the system. To say the least, I didn't make many friends at the Birmingham airport and I was reminded one more time just how much I hate those terrorists who have escalated these frustrating measures of security and safety.

The flight did grant me the pleasure of sitting beside NASCAR legend Bobby Allison. He's got a really cool watch with the band consisting of gold-plated racecars. I told you it was cool! Our landing was a tad rough and he uttered, "Came in a little hot on that one." He wasn't scared of the speed but he definitely noticed it.

PARENTAL WISDOM REVEALED

I was amazed at how much smarter I immediately became as soon as I entered the blessed membership of fatherhood. Well, maybe 'smart' is not the most accurate word---more like 'wise.' Now, I'm not suggesting that I hold the title of necessarily being smart or wise, but for sure, I am now wiser. And all because I simply had kids!

There are so many things you learn being on this side of discipline. And by "this side," I mean the giving it, not receiving it. As we all heard growing up when we got scolded and "naughty chaired" by our moms and dads, they'd utter every time, "This is going to hurt me more than it's going to hurt you." And as a little feller on the receiving end, I'm sure my thoughts represented every child elsewhere throughout the entire world who was getting in trouble at that very time: *Yeah right! How can anything hurt worse than being disciplined by Mom and Dad?* Boy was I wrong! You other parents out there know what I'm talking about. We have to do it. It's in our job description to be a good parent to our kids.

But if my little girl would ask me if she could juggle chainsaws while standing on a barbed wire fence barefooted, I'd have to think about it---anything to stave off the idea of telling her "no" and risk hurting her feelings! But I do tell both of mine "no," "don't do it again," don't make me come back there," and the ever useful and effective "I'm going to count to three."

The most popular "because I'm your dad, that's why," is one I don't subscribe to. I'm one who likes to have reason to my questions and arguments and this one doesn't offer it at all. For me, being a dad is a blessing, not a reason. It certainly could work in certain situations, but I wouldn't appreciate it if I asked my son why he just threw his sister's pants off the balcony and he came back with, "because I'm your son, that's why." See, it just doesn't offer much.

But here's where you need to get your pen and paper out to take some notes. I'm about to reveal the one statement that possesses and encompasses all the wisdom and power of every parent that there has ever been. And it's something you don't learn, or rather realize, until you become a parent. This statement to which I'm referring is "I told you so." Who knew four little words could be so powerful? This phrase only needs to be said once and then its effectiveness is released in every situation that a parent will participate in forevermore.

Here's how it works. A child is doing something as simple and innocent as running through the house chasing a ball. His mother says, "Be careful or you're going to hurt yourself." Now if this child continues to run through the house for six consecutive light years and never even so as much stumps his toe, the mother can then be seen as merely being cautious. No big deal because nobody got hurt. It's a safeguard that never needed to be cashed in. But, as soon as this child nicks his elbow on a doorjamb, the mother now has every right to entirely and completely exercise the phrase "I told you so." And so it begins.

And the reason this works so well is because no one likes to hear from somebody else "I told you so." Even if we knew better to start with and even if it's from our own mom and dad. We like to think that no one knows our actions and decisions better than ourselves. *Even* if we are only 18 months old and are completely incapable of deciphering Order and Reason.

So the next time when you kids are doing something that suggests the slightest margin of error could potentially be involved, and your parents offer the caring advice of "be careful" or "are you sure that's the best thing to do?", for heaven's sake, be careful because now the "I told you so" philosophy has been introduced and, well, quite frankly, it probably *isn't* the best thing for you to do. And you know what happens if you don't listen to me? I told you so.

REMEMBER, DON'T FORGET TO REMEMBER

Do you remember where you were on the night of June 29th six years ago? What about the eighteenth President of the United States? No, not where he was on the 29th; I mean who was he? How about what you wore to church last Sunday? Or what about what you had for dinner last night? Don't worry, if you answered "I don't know" to any of these, then you're average. If you answered, "I have no idea," then congratulations, you're considered normal.

Well, I don't like to think that I'm anywhere near the title of "getting old" but I do know that I ain't gettin' any younger. Between my wife and my two little growing tricycle motors, they're doing a pretty good job in turning some brown hairs grey and killing a few memory cells. This is true! I can't remember things like I used to. Sometimes I can't remember if I fed Boomer or not. And I bet I spend close to ten minutes a day searching for my wallet and keys. But leave it up to those smart fellas in white labcoats who work up in those fancy buildings in D.C., you know, the ones with Modern Science engraved on marble out front; now those guys have come up with some help. That's right, something to help us keep our 'remembering' cells strong. It's a vitamin, well, it's actually an herbal dose, well, let's call it a pill, okay, I'm not sure what you categorize it as, but it's called Ginkgo Biloba.

I'm sure ya'll have probably heard about this herbal vitamin pill dosage. I remember the first time I went in to Wal-Mart and asked for it. I asked them if they had any

Geico Balboa. That lady pharmacist looked at me funny. I said, "Yeah, you know, it's green and it grows on Chinese trees---it's called Bingo Wan Ben Kenobi." Then I confessed that I couldn't remember what it was called and that was the main reason for me getting it; was to help me remember. She knew immediately what I was talking about then and handed me the bottle and slowly pronounced G-I-N-G-K-O B-I-L-O-B-A. I agreed with her and said, "Yeah, that's what I said."

I think that's pretty good marketing right there, though. Some people got in a room and said let's come up with a pill that helps your memory but give it a big funny name that people can't remember. This way when people go and ask for it and can't remember what it's called, then they'll really feel like they need it.

Well, I've been taking it for about three months now and I have tell you, I haven't yet lost my wallet and Boomer's dish is always full. Yes, my wife has been feeding Boomer and she bought me a chain for my wallet, but still, I'm remembering to take my Plinko Wasabi pills! That counts for something, doesn't it?

My granddaddy used to sleep on his back, wear loose shoes, drink two cups of coffee a day and chew on a pinch of catnip. He lived to be eighty-nine and *never* forgot anything. I ain't chewing no catnip but I will wear bigger shoes.

WOW! A LOOSE TOOTH!

"Wow! Sweetie, that tooth is really loose! Don't wiggle it too much because it might come out."

"But, Daddy isn't that why we get loose tooths? So they'll come out and make room for better ones?"

I hate it when I get bested in a simple conversation by a four year-old! It doesn't do much for the supposed big-time SuperDaddy image. I thought parents were supposed to know everything. I knew my teachers did: they had bright red pens to prove it. But c'mon, where's that elusive copy of *The International Parents Handbook: How to be Smarter Than Your Child or At Least Seem To Be So He or She Won't Know the Difference*. It would have come in handy when I got asked *so how do we really know that all snowflakes are different?* Or *why does Porky Pig wear pants?* Or my favorite *does God have fingernails?*

Now I applaud the inquisitive nature but you're killing me here. I've tried the always useful "diversion tactic." But kids don't forget. And if they asked, it's because they want to know. This parenting thing is tricky. I thought it was all downhill once I learned how to change diapers!

Let me un-digress back to what I digressed from. The loose tooth. Let me come right out and say that I don't have any idea why God thought it was a good idea for kids not to just be born with a full set of teeth. Teething years are *not* fun. And then, once this painful and challenging time is over with, what's the reward? Lose them! At least our memory was not fully developed enough to remember how "inconvenient" getting our teeth was. But boy, do I remember my first loose tooth.

And when my daughter first wiggled her lower central incisor at me, that twisting pit in my stomach haunted me immediately. I remember, back when, trying to make sense of why this tooth became loose. I mean, our ears don't fall off and we grow new ones, right? Our nose doesn't fall off and we grow a better one that doesn't need blowing? Will my feet come off one day and I'll replace them with ones that make me run faster? The answer is obviously no to all of these, so why do we lose our teeth?

I had to know if this was normal so I went to the smarter person I knew at the time: my big brother. He's been here, done this, right? He just chuckled at me, rolled his eyes (as only big brothers can do) and said, "Don't worry about it. It'll come out. But if it doesn't, you'll have to tie a string around it and the other end to a doorknob and shut the door really fast. This'll bring it out." My fear level elevated to orange.

So you can see why I don't like loose teeth. I was trying to comfort her fear, falsely assuming it was the same as mine. I immediately offered something to hopefully dispel the dread of "tie a string around it" or the classic "off like a band-aid" maneuver. I threw Logic and Reason out the window and somehow managed to bypass the bigger idea that that's just how God wants it to be. And it backfired on me.

So the tooth came out and all is well. Well, almost. Now it's time to call on the Tooth Fairy. Several questions arose. First, who came up with this little imaginary tusky imp? Second, under your pillow? Why not the nightstand or in the middle of your floor? Or better yet, just leave the tooth outside your door like a hotel breakfast order? And third, what's the going rate for a tooth these days? I got a shiny quarter but that was almost thirty years ago. Is a dollar too much or does it fall short of what the other kids are getting? Is there a formula somewhere to plug in the numbers to account for inflation plus time plus the consumer price index? And don't forget, we're in some challenging economic times, too. I just can't be sneaking in rooms leaving dollar bills under pillows every month. And why *does* Porky Pig wear pants? I don't know!

Who thought a loose tooth could bring on such questions and worries to a man who just needed to say, "Wow!" That's all kids want to hear. Just *wow!*

LAWS PASSED? I PASSED THE LAW!

I just got a ticket. Not a ticket to the Final Four or the Circus. I mean *the* ticket. A speeding ticket. But because I still had two more hours on the highway after the cop slapped my knuckles, I had plenty of thinking time. And during this period of reflection, I came up with a new law that I'm going to run by my congressman. The name of the law I'm proposing is LOUSE WRITTLE BOPHARS. It's an acronym, people! I'll explain in a minute.

First, let me set the stage. I was driving down the highway, the radio turned off and I was actually enjoying my drive for once as there were no impending vehicles in the rear view mirror. And then in a matter of seconds it seemed, that empty rear view filled up with two trucks, a SUV, three cars and four tractor trailers! Where'd they come from? And then when I looked back through the windshield, that Subaru Justy that was a whole mile marker ahead of me was now sputtering exhaust on my fog lights! In other words, if this were a peanut butter sandwich, I was the peanut butter and *not* the bread!

I checked the left lane and saw this parade of speed racers coming on strong, so I made the decision to pass the Justy and slide back over comfortably in the right lane again and let the parade pass. So I did just that. And would you believe that at the very moment of passing that annoying little Subaru, I also passed a perfectly placed state trooper with radar. Oh yeah, and it was just about 45 seconds later that my fears were confirmed and my stomach dropped down in my kneecaps. As the Snowman once told the Bandit, "Son, you got a Texas bubble gum machine on your tail!" And I did.

Well, you know the drill from here on out. License, registration, sit tight, fill out ticket, uncomfortable trooper small talk, a stupid non-funny joke in desperate attempt to get just a warning, nice try, court date and drive careful. And all this took right at twenty minutes. Seriously, twenty minutes that I'll never get back because some trooper, who I, by the way, contribute to his salary, was out making our highways a safer place to travel by doing his job by busting some zealous "concrete sailors" who are exceeding the speed limit and jeopardizing the lives of others around them! I want him to do his job, but leave me out of it!

Anyway, here's where my new law is going to come in handy. It has to do with that twenty minutes when I was sitting idly on the side of the road. That's precious time. And precious time wasted! See, here's the main problem: I got busted for speeding but that's probably because I had a pretty good reason for my excessive speed. First it was that Justy slowing me down and now it's this trooper. Don't get me wrong, it's not the trooper's fault, it's all mine. But I need to get this twenty minutes back somehow. And when I pulled back into the interstate race again, the first thing I thought about is "Man, I need to make up some time here." But I can't! I just got busted for that! Unless Congress passes LOUSE WRITTLE BOPHARS.

LOUSE WRITTLE BOPHARS stands for Law Of Unforeseen Safety Ensuement Which Reimburses Initial Total Time Lapsed Enforced By Officers Patrolling Highway And Road Systems. This law would allow and grant the fresh ticket holder the right to excessively speed for the exact amount of time that he spent idly on the side of the road getting his ticket. So, since it took me and

Roscoe P. Coltrane twenty minutes to process my ticket, then I get twenty minutes to speed and make up for the time wasted. Need some more convincing?

By passing this law, it would encourage people to speed, therefore more tickets, therefore more money for the state, therefore travelers would get to where they're going quicker, therefore making our highways ultimately safer because travelers aren't spending as much time on them because they're getting to their destinations faster. Makes sense, don't it? Once I get this jewel passed, I'm probably going to run for Senator or something like that. Don't worry, I'll let you put one of my signs in your yard. Until then, keep the pedal to the metal!

SPRING HAS SPRUNG

March is over, April is among us, and Easter is nigh. And, oh yeah, spring has sprung. Thank goodness for Christmas or winter wouldn't have a fighting chance with the other three seasons. The only thing to look forward to after December 25th is a really big snowfall. I'm not talking about a light dusting that looks like the sky has a dandruff problem; I'm talking about the clouds letting loose. Snow piled so high that when people in Antarctica see it on the news, they get jealous!

But since this didn't happen, bring on some Spring. It has been said that spring is the "rebirth" season. Dry patchy brown spots in the yard suddenly sprout plushy green hairs of forgotten grass. Those fleece pullovers and wool sweaters we've been donning for the last five months are turned in for golf shirts and pastel sundresses. We can now crack open a window and comfortably leave it open till evening. A fresh breeze has never been more welcomed. Birds of all kind seem to dance on the branches of budding trees, whistling rhythmic patterns that come so close to a sing-able melody. Wicker furniture reappears on newly swept patios. Flower pots are overflowing with a compilation of flowers that splash and dazzle the eye of a once dreary and gloomy morning. And almanacs are referenced to determine when to plant the first stages of a garden, just waiting for a warm ground and the last frost.

But nothing says "Spring is here!" more than Easter. I've always viewed Easter as the second New Year. It's another chance to change those habits I promised to kick January 1st but reluctantly picked back up just a quick week later. It's so hard to change yourself when nothing else around you is changing. To me, that's why New Year's resolutions never work. Easter is God's way of saying to us, "Okay, I'll change the weather, the scenery, your wardrobe and you won't get shocked every time you open a door." Now this is change I can live with and change I can change for. Easter is time for another chance for me to recommit, rededicate, and re-promise things I should have done already.

Plus, Easter is the only major holiday that floats on the calendar. It's determined every year to be celebrated on the first Sunday after the Paschal Full Moon, or in other words, the first moon whose 14th day is on or after the ecclesiastic vernal equinox. Are we clear? What all this means to me, is that Easter itself is always changing. What better time to recreate and change our lives than with a holiday that is constantly changing, too!

And it wasn't a coincidence that God hung his Son on a cross one Spring morning 2000 years ago. It was His promise to us that we would be reborn in his grace and mercy. Easter is a time to get excited again about the very things that make us happy and comfortable. It's the Grand Opening to the rest of the year. Not the first Grand Opening, but a second one. One that lets us catch up and start over again. A second chance for all of us, in more ways than one.

THANK A SOLDIER

A few years back, I had the privilege of substitute teaching at a local high school. I quickly learned that a lot had changed from the decade ago when I graduated. And even though I was the one who was deemed as the "teacher", during one short hour, I became a student and learned one of the more important lessons I still carry with me to this day. And especially on this Memorial Day's weekend.

About ten minutes before the ringing of the first period bell, I caught a glimpse of a figure in the hall who walked by the door. He wore a tight haircut covered mostly by a slanted beret, sand-colored work boots that touched his kneecaps, matching camouflaged pants and jacket, and he strutted confidently with a commanding and intimidating presence that demanded your respect. And his face, just a little bit older, reminded me of that guy who used to sit two tables over from me at lunch in this same high school cafeteria. Nonetheless, no matter who he was, he definitely seemed out of place, which explained why everyone else who saw him was staring, too.

After the bell rang, I walked across the hall to talk to my friend who is a history teacher. He knew I didn't have a class the next period, so he invited me to come and sit in with his class as they were having a special guest speaker.

The class was rowdy knowing that any workbook activity planned for this period was postponed due to their speaker. In walked this figure and a hush fell immediately over them. The uniform, the odd-shaped hat, the gait, and that look. His face was still youthful but his look was seasoned with experience, challenges, quick decision-making and had stared the reality of death in the face a few times.

He spoke to those kids for the next hour about his time in Iraq and all the good and progress that had taken place and was continuing to take place. He explained to them that war is real; it's not fun and sometimes is necessary for the better sake of others who are not as fortunate, strong or free as we are. Just the same as the rich help the poor and the strong help the weak, the free help the shackled.

One boy in the back of the class raised his hand and said, "You've told us all the things you've done for us. So what can we do for you?"

The soldier never skipped a beat. "Just thank us. We serve because we want to and we care about others. So show that you care about us by thanking us. That's it."

As it turned out, I did go to school with him and I remember staring into his face as we matched up in intramural basketball games. I remember laughing with him on graduation night. And now I was staring into that same face thinking of the things he's accomplished in the name of betterment and safety for our country.

I've read *The Red Badge of Courage* and have seen *Saving Private Ryan*, but listening to this classmate share his patriotism and solemn duties with that class brought the realism home for me.

That day, those kids learned how to respect and support the brave men and women who serve and protect them in ways we will never know about. That day, I found a new level of admiration and upped my ante of appreciation for every soldier since then. Whether I'm at the mall, the airport, a baseball game or the post office, I take a mere five seconds out of my free life to walk to that soldier, shake his or her hand, look them in the eye and say "Thanks for your service." Of all they do for me, even this quick gesture, and a small one by comparison, rekindles that great American spirit that has always and will always bond us together. Memorial Day was created to commemorate the men and women who have died while in the military service. I say we thank a soldier while we can before it's too late.

WHEN DID WAVING GO OUT OF STYLE?

I have a friend who has a theory that the beginning of the great fall of our culture of orderly composure and established civilization as we know it, is put into motion by anyone who owns a pickup truck. Stay with me---I'll explain. His theory goes like this: Guy buys truck. Friends find out that he now owns a truck. Friends use truck to move stuff. Stuff moved is either taken to Goodwill, the dump, storage or the basement of a newly purchased bigger house. Friends now need more stuff. Friends call on truck owner to take them to Wal-Mart. And that's what's wrong with the world today: everybody's up at Wal-Mart!

I know, it's a leftfield attempt at not only trying to solve the world's problems, but even trying to figure out what they are. Nonetheless, just about every conversation he and I have, one of us invariably will come around to uttering the phrase, "...and that's what's wrong with the world today!" I know you've been in some of these conversations, too. And even if you've never said that phrase, I know you've at least thought it. We all, no matter how old or young, can remember back to our "the good ol' days." It's funny how we say we look forward to tomorrow, but all we really want is one more yesterday.

There are many things that we may attribute to the decay of what once was good and better---they're all debatable as to which has contributed to it more. Could be the "left lane mentality" of those who can't even wait 3 seconds to receive their email. Could be that no one is accountable for anything anymore. Could be the idea that we're becoming way too soft in not allowing failure and losing to be a part of the formula for success and winning. Maybe it's that we traded in ties and aprons for tattoos and halter tops. Or it could've been when we started rounding our change to the nearest dollar.

I'm not completely sure which one it is; it changes daily. But I have noticed one thing in particular that snaps my belt loops. It's a small thing, one that requires minimal effort, costs nothing, has no political affiliation and when demonstrated properly, cannot offend even the most sensitive and petty. It's waving. Yes, a simple wave. People either don't know how to do it anymore or they don't recognize it. I thought waving to people, especially in the south, ranked right up there with drinking sweet tea and rooting for Richard Petty.

Whether it's allowing someone to merge over a lane in traffic or you've made eye contact with someone a second longer than is comfortable, a simple wave takes care of both situations. Now our mommas told us not to talk to strangers, and especially to strange people, but I don't recall anything about the nicety brought about through the form of a simple gesture relaying the message of "hello" or "thank you."

I've had people wrinkle their foreheads and furrow their brows and come close to a full blown scowl when I have waved at them. I understand someone having a bad day or they don't know me, but a reciprocal hand in the air can't hurt that much, can it?

Sometimes, I get in the truck and ride a few miles out to find a gravel road, roll my window down and just wave at strangers for no reason at all. I'll wave at them, then they wave back at me and then the whole cycle suddenly stops when somebody flags me down, runs up to my truck and asks for a lift to Wal-Mart!

MY TIME AT FORT CAMPBELL

I, along with two other friends and entertainers, had the gracious honor and privilege to visit and perform at the United States Army Post at Fort Campbell, Kentucky. We were invited there to perform a Christmas play with music, laughs and stories for anyone and everyone on the post. Because I have the sincerest love for our country and the utmost gratitude and respect for those men and women and their families who sacrifice so much of their lives to grant and protect our freedoms, I wanted to take a minute to let you know what a wonderful experience this was for us. God bless every one of them.

From the guard who checked our ID at the gate to the stagehands who jumped in and unloaded equipment (and also stood in the wings and made faces at us during the show!) to the ladies who made popcorn in the theater lobby to the kids who laughed and giggled at three strangely dressed Santa Clauses sittin' 'round a toeroaster to the generals and colonels sitting on the front row finding an escape in an open-mouthed smile from their daily military concerns, we can safely say that everyone had a blast! God bless every one of them.

We were surrounded by 30,000 of the finest that this country has to offer and couldn't have felt more at home if we were sitting in our own worn out La-Z-Boys. Fort Campbell is the third largest post in the U.S and is home of the 101st Airborne. These guys are the first line of any military conflict or situation that needs to be remedied according to our Department of Defense. Basically this means that when you read about some kind of U.S. military involvement on your Yahoo homepage, these guys have already been there for about thirty-six hours taking care of it. God bless every one of them.

Our audience was made up military mommies, daddies and kids who were gearing up for Christmas and all in a glee from the recent return of those mommies and daddies who had been gone for the past 18 months. I know how it is, certainly on a smaller scale, to be away from your family and loved ones and how joyous it is to return, especially at Christmas! There's nothing sweeter in the world, especially at Christmas time, than a mother and father who glow with pride by simply watching their child lose himself in laughter, and, of course, a child's genuine and unexpected giggle that lights up an entire room. God bless every one of them.

After our show, we were presented with a Certificate of Appreciation by Garrison Commander Swope. A very special gesture on his behalf and we thank him for all he does. And then backstage, we were quickly corralled to a dimly lit corner where a One Star General, Brig. GEN Rife, stood commandingly in his fatigues. He talked very matter-of-factly and his demeanor was succinct and demanded your attention and respect. He thanked us for being there and sharing our talents and message with all those in attendance. And then he turned to each one of us, stared us in the eye and held out a Screaming Eagles Coin Of Excellence in the palm of his hand. He then shook our hands, transferring the coin to our own sweaty palms. And just as quickly as our encounter had begun, it ended the same, with him turning and ultimately returning to his higher duties of National Security. Our meeting was quick but nonetheless, a humbling moment we will never forget and will gladly tell again and again. We quietly went back to our dressing room and all the while that we were changing our clothes, we all three were eerily silent, still soaking up what we had just been a small part of. God bless these men in all that they do.

The irony was not lost; this One Star General thanking *us* and giving *us* a token of "excellence". Our thanks are tenfold to him and all those who match his excellence in their service. Again, we were, still are and always will be sincerely honored by all those of whom we encountered that memorable day on the post. We got to see a first-hand glimpse of what sacrifices and realities our fellow Americans, good down-home hard-working guys and gals, just like me and you, live through daily. Say a prayer of thanks for their service and for their safety. God bless every one of them.

GIVING THANKS FOR THANKSGIVING

We're all familiar with that beautiful picture painted by Norman Rockwell in 1943 titled *Freedom From Want*. It's the one where the grandmother is setting that perfectly cooked turkey on the table in the midst of her finer special occasion china. There are about four different joyous conversations taking place and the gentleman in the lower right corner is peering around as if to invite you personally to pull up a chair. And everything from the aged wallpaper in the background to the fact that Grandpa is wearing a coat and tie for the blessed dinner to the interesting idea of everyone having water to drink or, just the overall happiness that the whole family is together, this picture puts us right where we want to be. There are so many reasons for us to appreciate and relate to this stereotypical scene of Americana. The alternate title for this painting is aptly *Thanksgiving Dinner*. And whenever someone mentions the phrase "Thanksgiving dinner", this image is immediately what my mind calls up. And immediately I begin to smile. Because it is a wonderful image.

Now upon deeper thought and insight, maybe the reason I love this picture so much is because it takes me back to a simpler time. (And this family was painted some 32 years *before* my simpler time began!) Maybe it's because when I see it, I long to be home again for a long weekend from college. Maybe it's that it reminds me of those homemade dinner smells that used to come from Grandma's kitchen that, sadly, I don't get to enjoy anymore. Or maybe it's just because I really like turkey! Again, there are numerous reasons we can find to fall in love with this time and setting and, of course, this special day.

But here's the most beautiful part about this picture: it's still going on today. That's right, Thanksgiving is alive and well, and best of all, untouched. Thanksgiving is the same today as it was in 1950. And as it was in 1900. It's basically the same as it was in 1621. Those Plymouth settlers, or as they became known, the Pilgrims, sat down with the Wampanoag Indians and celebrated the fruits of their autumn harvest, hugged one another and gave an ever grateful plaudit to God for all that they had enjoyed and endured. And then they ate and they drank and became merry. This sounds like the perfect kind of celebration to me.

Now you might be thinking to yourself right now: Big deal. There are about 100 other holidays throughout the year that have been going on a long time, too. What's so special about this one? Well, it goes back to the word mentioned earlier: Thanksgiving is untouched. It hasn't been dominated by commercialism, or stained with secularism or tainted by the demand of different cultures. Now sure, the Butterball Turkey people see a spike in their sales at the end of November and the Cowboys and Lions weren't playing football in the Plymouth Rock Stadium, but the true meaning of this day is still sacred. Candy and flowers have taken over Valentines Day, the Easter Bunny is more noticed than sunrise services, and Santa Claus sometimes seems to overshadow a Savior's birth, but Thanksgiving remains to be about family, food and gratitude. This is what it has always been about. It remains wholesome. It remains in its intended form. It remains untouched.

Don't get me wrong, as I'm not complaining about how these other holidays have branched with other traditions and marketing focus. I love these holidays for those reasons, too, and for what they are and ultimately what they've come to be. Seriously, I overly patronize Russell Stover, buy 30 packs of marshmallow peeps and use Jolly Old St. Nick to bargain year-long disciplinary tactics on little ones at my house! It's just that there is a sincere reverence that is beheld with the family on Thanksgiving Day.

And the intent of Thanksgiving is so pure and simple. What a great idea; let's come together and say thanks for all that we have and know and all that's good. President George Washington said it perfectly in 1789 when he issued a National Thanksgiving Proclamation: "Now therefore I do recommend and assign Thursday the 26th day of November next to be devoted by the People of these States to the service of that great and glorious Being, who is the beneficent Author of all the good that was, that is, or that will be—That we may then all unite in rendering unto Him our sincere and humble thanks—for His kind care and protection of the People of this Country...for the signal and manifold mercies, and the favorable interpositions of His Providence which we experienced in the tranquility, union, and plenty, which we have since enjoyed..."

Amen, Mr. President. Amen.

It's become a somewhat widespread tradition throughout homes across America where families sit around the table on this holiday and take a turn saying something that they're thankful for. Again, a very pure and simple action. Well, this year as I sit in front of Mom's finer china and a platter full of tryptophan, I believe that I will have that Rockwell picture burned in my brain, I'll raise a glass to Squanto and proclaim my list of things that I'm thankful for. And I'm pretty sure I know what I'm going to end my list with this year. Of course, there will be my family who loves me, the friends who support me, the good health that I enjoy, those who have and are currently fighting to protect all my freedoms, the knowledge which leads to understanding, the opportunities given, the luxuries that I know, the food that I am about to eat and that I'm a gracious recipient of God's good providence. And one more thing; I'm thankful for Thanksgiving.

I LOVE OLD PEOPLE

I've reached that age that when I recall my high school days, they're not as bad as I used to think they were. For the longest time, I remember thinking that I couldn't wait to graduate and be on my own. Now I'm at that age that I often wish I was that homework-laden non-billpaying senior getting nervous about prom.

I've reached that age that when someone asks me about a certain event that happened in my life, I respond with an "Oh yeah, that was just four or five years ago." Actually, that event happened closer to 14 to 15 years ago!

I've reached that age that when I see a TV show on Nick-At-Nite, I remember enjoying it the *first* time it ran.

I've reached that age that when I talk to a familiar looking little tyke in the grocery store, I start the conversation with "You know, I went to school with your father." I never thought my classmates I used to cruise the avenue with would grow up and be fathers! Fathers? Fathers are old! Not old in a bad way, just old in an older way.

And I've also reached that age that when my wife and I find a sitter for a Friday night, we wind up at Lowe's picking out paint to finish off the basement. I know, don't get jealous---it's pretty exciting stuff!

But getting older doesn't bother me---well, not as much as I think it should. Who knows, as I get older, it may. Personally, I enjoy older people. And I don't mean to use the word "old" to describe a particular age---just someone

139

who is seasoned, far beyond their salad years, and got some dirt in the cracks of their hands. You know who you are.

They entertain the devil out of me. To me, they seem to have their entire life story written on their face. What you see is what you get with them. Every wrinkle, gesture and quip is their honesty, experience and judgment just seeping out of them. They don't hold back any part of anything they're thinking. They'll tell you like it is without any regard to whether it might offend you and they don't bow down to the almighty and ever-present looming idea of PC-ness. I love this! I wish more people were like this. As a matter of fact, I can't wait to be like them one day.

Today, the younger generation, or the kids, as I like to call them, are so unpredictable. They want to shock you with piercings and clothes that don't fit and bumper stickers on their cars that don't make any sense. And if I did understand those stickers, it would probably scare me. Any issues that kids have today, they just mask it with an image of somebody whom they want you to think they are. I understand fads and fashions and styles that may not pertain to me, but putting an extra effort in to being strange and weird and somebody who you really are not, is something I just don't get. I know, they're all just searching their souls trying to find themselves, but I got to tell you, I can't wait for that glorious day to arrive.

I think that's what's so great about old people: they've found themselves and are completely comfortable with it. And by golly, if you don't like it, well then you're just going to have to find some way to deal with it. And there's never anything imposing about it; it is just what it is and they are just who they are. And they only tell you if you ask.

So I'm all for the youth of today being the foundation of tomorrow and all that, but I applaud the "old people." And believe me, with each passing day, I'm well on my way to becoming just like you.

STRANGE LAWS

I'm curious by nature. Maybe I get it from my philosophical studies. Maybe from reading a lot of Socrates. Or maybe from my bedtime stories of Curious George. I don't think it matters, I just know that I am. And I'm pretty sure you are, too.

While doing some research for another project, I recently came across a law in Ohio declaring that if you ignore an orator on Decoration Day to such an extent as to publicly play croquet or pitch horseshoes within one mile of the speakers' stand, you can be fined $25. After reading this, I must say that my nature of curiosity was piqued. I then read on and found a slew of outlandish laws that are actually still on the books today in some states and countries. They were obviously made in a different time under older-fashioned situations. I picked out my favorite 15 and wanted to share them with you---not only for entertainment value but for you to keep in mind when visiting these places so that you may be a law abiding citizen and not land yourself in jail for simply not knowing.

- In Wilbur, Washington it is illegal to ride an ugly horse.

And in Oklahoma you can be arrested for making ugly faces at a dog. *But what if that horse looks at the dog?*

- In Vancouver, British Columbia the speed limit for tricycles is 10 miles per hour. *So...for a unicycle I guess its speed limit is 3.33 mph.*

- In Athens, Greece driving on public roads while unbathed or poorly dressed can cost you your driver's license. *Note to Nick Nolte: don't go to Athens.*

- In Idaho, you can't fish on a camel's back. You can't roller skate in a buffalo herd, either.

- In New York, the penalty for jumping off a building is death. *Uhh....duh.*

- It's illegal to chain an alligator to a fire hydrant in Michigan. *That's why I always chain my alligators to parking meters.*

- In Florida, if an elephant is left tied to a parking meter, the parking fee has to be paid just as it would for a vehicle. *That's why I always tie my elephants to fire hydrants.*

- It is illegal to die in the Britain Houses of Parliament. *Aside from not living anymore, it's just plain rude.*

- In Haifa, Israel it is forbidden to bring bears to the beach. You can take them to Wal-Mart and the playground, but no beach!

- In Washington, it is mandatory for a motorist with criminal intentions to stop at the city limits and telephone the chief of police as he is entering the town. *Well, this makes perfect sense due to the high rate of honest criminals we have out there.*

- West Virginia children may not attend school with their breath smelling of "wild onions." *That's why they have garlic-scented toothpaste.*

- A man can be arrested for wearing a skirt in Italy. *So that's why RuPaul never vacations there.*

- In Tennessee, it is illegal to use a lasso to catch a fish. *I'd post this man's bail just to see this feat.*

- In Raton, New Mexico it is illegal for a woman to ride horseback down a public street with a kimono on. *So it's legal for her to ride with her kimono off?*

And finally...
In Samoa, it's a crime to forget your wife's birthday.

Not just in Samoa, buddy!

DARBY'S HASSLE

I think it's time to educate you, you know, the hard working people of the country, about a fiscal situation gone awry. Now fiscal is just a high dollar word meaning monetary and monetary is just a longer word meaning money. And anytime somebody talks about money, people listen. So I hope you're listening, because I'm about to tell you a way that you can save money! That's right, keep money in your pocket. But hang with me a bit; it's going to sound strange at first.

So my lovely and I are in the truck and she tells me that she's hungry. I pulled through the drive-thru of this famous fast-food place---I'll make up a name to protect the guilty---let's call this place, um...aw, I don't know...how about Darby's. I rolled down the window and was now in a conversation with a sixteen-year old girl who obviously didn't care about anything else in this world except who's going to be at the high school football game Friday night. And I could tell all this just by listening to her coming through a rusty speaker that didn't half work. My wife told me that she only wanted a roast beef and a medium diet drink. When I relayed this order to my teeny-bopper friend, she politely responded, "So you want a Number 1?"

To catch you up here, a Number 1 is exactly what my wife wanted, but with fries. So I answered, "Sure, that's fine. I'll take the Number 1."

I was quickly alerted with a slap on the shoulder that she didn't want the Number 1 because of the fries. I then had to ask, "What's wrong with fries?"

"They're a Code Red for my swimsuit, that's what! Fries go straight to my thighs! I love them! That's why I don't want them. I'm reducing temptation!" So I told the little girl in the speaker that I just wanted the sandwich and the drink.

"But sir," she said, "A sandwich and drink will cost you $4.93, but the Number 1 Combo Meal will cost you $4.17. You get more for less."

"True, but I also get less for more. I don't think that's right."

"We try to focus on the positive here, sir."

Well why don't they focus on *exactly* what I want! I saw where this game of chicken, or I guess I should say roast beef, could've gone on all day long. Now I was faced with keeping the little lady happy by not ordering the fries or, giving in to the almighty fast-food combination value meal economics. Talking 'bout being 'tween a rock and a hard place!

At first, I froze. Then, I took a deep breath and committed. "I'll take the Number 1." I pulled around to the window and I paid the $4.17. I handed my lovely her sandwich and drink. And then as I pulled out on to the big road, I threw the fries out the window.

She gasped in shock and blurted out, "What are you doing?"

I calmly said, "Reducing your temptation and saving me seventy six cents."

I don't necessarily encourage throwing food out your car window, but if it saves you money and keeps you from sleeping on the couch, then why not?

SUMMER CAMP

We're all right up in the middle of summer and we're juggling schedules and carpooling to camps. It's challenging sometimes to find that reasonable balance of having your kids "take it easy" and "keep them busy" during the summer. We want them to take that much needed break from the hard schoolwork but then we worry that their minds will go stale and get dusty if it's not exercised enough during the down time.

And this is where a good camp comes to the rescue. It's long enough to satiate that hunger to keep them from starving on boredom and it's short enough to where it doesn't feel like school or a job.

I remember when I was a kid and hearing about these camps that others were going to. I didn't think much of them. And here's why. When I heard the word "camp", I just assumed that that meant someone was going to be shipped out in the middle of the George Washington National Forest with a tent, a rusty thermos and bug repellent. Have fun! I really thought that anytime someone went to camp, it was in the woods, there were grizzly bears all around and you had to go outside at night to use the bathroom. And that meant that not only was nature calling but so were the grizzlies.

I knew about hunting camps. All of them were hot, sticky and I usually left with poison ivy. In short, let me just say there are not a lot of producers on the Outdoor Network looking to ask me to host their next show. I do love being outdoors, but if I'm going "camping" then there's going to be a TV and a continental breakfast involved somehow.

But then one day, one of my childhood friends mentioned he was going to baseball camp. Baseball camp? I love baseball. But camp? I thought *you can't learn to turn a double play inside of a tent?* Obviously, it was something totally different and my world opened up to a newfound love of this camp idea. We played baseball for five hours everyday with other kids who loved the game just as much as I did. I learned and played and learned some more.

I'm sure all of us have attended some camp of some sort along the way. I'm glad to see that there are so many being offered and available to kids in our area. There are volleyball and science and art and swimming and karate camps. And fishing and music and vacation Bible schools. All of these are wonderful resources to keep kids involved, learning and growing into the talented young products that will ultimately impact their lives and maybe even impact ours in a new and better way.

So thanks to all those coordinators, counselors and volunteers who offer their time and skills to these kids and who are making a difference. If you have kids, enroll them in one. If you don't have kids, volunteer for one. And if you can't make either of these happen, just support them with a simple thank you to those who are stepping up and playing a role for the upcoming generation.

FUNDAMENTALLY SPEAKING

Some 31 years ago, I was standing in some brand new Converse hightops on that rubberized basketball court of the YMCA. It was the first day of learning one of the sports that still provides me my minimum quota of weekly exercise today. Coaches were barking the basics of the game to us. *Dribble with one hand. Bounce pass. Use the backboard.* Different coaches today still bark those same basic drills.

That same year I was introduced to America's Pastime. That first practice went a lot like that first basketball practice: different drills, same principles. *Keep your eye on the ball. Stay down on the grounders. Run out every hit. And use two hands to catch fly balls.* As I grew into this sport and honed my skills, I was ever so thankful to these coaches who made sure I knew the fundamentals of the game before going to the next level.

Jump ahead 12 years later. I'm sitting in a Calculus Math class wondering when in my life will I ever need to know how to find the derivative of an imaginary number. I was quickly told by my teacher, "This Friday on your test." So I began to put the basics of mathematics to use. I think I got a C on that test, but nonetheless, again I was thankful for those elementary teachers taking the time to show me the fundamentals of math: addition, subtraction, multiplication and division. And also to my English teachers so I could tell what a C looked like!

I could go on and on about how it is imperative if not impossible to learn the fundamentals of anything before we can actually put it to good use and advance ourselves to a better level with it. Whether it's construction, driving, parenting, typing, playing an instrument or plumbing. I feel confident in saying that we all agree we must know and learn the fundamentals. It doesn't matter about your religion, political party, skin color, IQ, what car you drive or whether you root for Tom or Jerry! No matter what we do, who we are and how good we do it, it all starts with the basics.

So last week I sat in my son's desk in his kindergarten room at a Back-to-School night. It doesn't get anymore fundamental than what's being introduced and taught in kindergarten. I sat there scanning the room, seeing lunchboxes, a nap mat, pencils, letters, numbers, colors, scissors, erasers, paper and disciplinary exercises on the chalkboard. The basics. Eat, sleep, write, count, cut, erase, and be good.

It then it hit me that we all get caught up in the complexities of life. And the topic of politics is the leader in this long list of complexities right now. In a span of two weeks, our tvs and headlines were saturated with each political party's heavy hitters carefully crafting their platitudes and promises of what they will and will not do. And sure, they have to do this, and we need for them to. But my head spins and my brain gets foggy and fuzzy trying to soak up stances on economic plans, healthcare options, foreign policy, employment opportunities, defense strategies, believe in America, yes we can and no they didn't. I think that the game of politics now is to just blur the basics. I find that usually when talking to someone, I am satisfied the most when I hear them say, "Basically, what I'm saying is..." That's all I want to know.

Basically. If I need more detail, I'll sign up for the newsletter!

The American entrepreneur, Jim Rohn, once said, "Success is the natural consequence of consistently applying the basic fundamentals." It doesn't get any clearer or truer than this simple approach. This beautiful little piece of philosophy should be on every month of every wall calendar with a picture of a crisp golden landscape scene to remind us all to strip down the complex and try on the simple again. Learn the fundamentals, know the fundamentals and apply the fundamentals. I'm reminded of this everyday I look at what my son is learning that day in school. Don't make it harder than it is.

And the first presidential candidate that holds his convention in a kindergarten classroom...oh yeah, he's got my vote!

RELIGION OF A DOG

I don't know who it was that said a dog is a man's best friend, but I'd cast my vote that he was the smartest man in the world.

If you're a cat person, sorry, you're probably not going to get much out of this one. But if you're a dog person, then you'll now exactly what I'm talking about.

Every Sunday night, I try to take some time and reflect on the minister's message and figure out how I can apply it to my life and ultimately how I can affect others with it. Be it my attitude, my actions, my reactions, learning to forgive quicker and easier, wear a broader smile, squash out negative thoughts, and to appreciate more of the good in the world than the bad. Looks good on paper and even pretty easy to say. But doing it? That's a whole different ball game. It's not that I can't do it, it's just getting those things to a point where they are a part of who I am and they become natural and involuntary.

And then I look at my dog.

He's been lying at my feet for the past hour as loyal as the day is long. Every now and again, he'll sit up and tilt his head back on my leg so I'll pinch his jowls and he is reassured that we are still friends.

When there's a knock at the door, he barks to let me know that someone is asking to enter my life and he wants to make sure that I am aware of them and don't miss that opportunity. When he hears an unusual noise outside, he also barks to alert me that something may be amiss and out of the ordinary. A pup's way of being cautious.

He drops his dirty tennis ball at my feet as a way of asking if we can play. And when I throw it across the yard and he catches it on the third bounce, he trots back prouder than punch waiting for a reward or a compliment as simple as "good boy!" And when he chases that squirrel into the woods, he realizes immediately that he has broken his boundaries and temptation got the better of him. He can't say "I'm sorry," but his sheepish walk around the patio and a tail tucked between his legs has never been mistaken for nothing less than an apology. A few harsh words of punishment and he retreats to his bed beside the fireplace knowing that he was wrong. Twenty minutes later and he'll sidle up beside me for a head rub to make sure that we're "cool" now.

It's a dog's nature to always want to be as pleasing to his master as he possibly can be. They can't read, they can't speak---but, oh, can they feel. If he feels scared, threatened or mad, he shows his teeth and offers a low growl. Good for him. He's got to protect himself; that just means he cares enough about himself to defend himself against something he doesn't like.

Now back to me sitting there on a Sunday night reflecting on the minister's message. Sometimes it's not a finely tuned sermon. Or a scholarly commentary offering up theological solutions for questions and concerns. Sometimes it just might be observing how my dog lives through life. The magical thing about a dog is that they seem to affect life, whereas life affects people. Dogs seem to make the situation better, instead of having the situation making them worse.

We've all seen that pillow that reads "I want to be the person that my dog thinks I am." If I could be the person I wanted to be *and* the one my dog thought I was, you couldn't stand to be in the same room with me!

ICE CREAM NIRVANA

"Laughter is the best medicine." We all know this quote and probably believe in it to a certain extent. It's a good one. Actually, I think it's a great one. Just about any or all uncomfortable or stressful or taxing situations can be dissolved with somebody prompting a laugh. I wouldn't recommend prompting that laugh at funerals, monasteries, or during Tiger's backswing, but all in all, laughing is a good thing.

If you're feeling down, laughing makes you feel better. If you're feeling up, then it's that much easier to laugh. We just have to be willing to find something funny in something to laugh at. Annie Fellows Johnston (whoever she was) once said that "men need laughter sometimes more than food." Very good point Ms. Fellows Johnston, however, au contraire. This brings me to my next and main point.

I confidently submit, due to avid, extensive, and consistent research, that this quotation, or mantra if you will (or even if you won't), shall be amended forevermore. Laughter is no longer the best medicine; it is ice cream.

Yes, at the bottom of all doctor prescription cards, it should read in bold letters: and be sure to consume daily, two scoops of your favorite ice cream to ensure the perfect balance of life that God has intended!

And don't cheat! Imitations aren't allowed. Popsicles are okay, but are not the real deal. And none of those knockoff overpriced French yogurts that catch your eye with pithy slogans like *tastes just like ice cream but healthier!* If you want to be happy and healthy, you've got to go for the real thing. No substitutes, preservatives or additives or alternatives. Ice cream, straight up.

If you're having a bad day, I dare you to try a scoop of Crazy Cotton Candy. Or Moosetracks with chocolate syrup. Or a Mocha Mountain Coco Blast with sprinkles. See if you don't immediately start feeling a little better. It's simple the way it works. Kids are happy. Kids like ice cream. When adults eat ice cream, it makes us feel like kids again. And when we feel like kids again, we're happy!

Come to think of it, I've never met anyone who doesn't like ice cream. I know those who don't like ice in their drinks and those who don't care for cream in their coffee; but never one who says, "I think I'll pass on the scoop of butter pecan with extra whip cream." I'd venture to bet that the next President of the United States could run on the campaign "I'm going to raise your taxes and slash your healthcare, but free ice cream for everyone!"

That candidate will win by a landslide.

I WANNA LIVE IN MAYBERRY

My favorite part of the evening is from 5:30 to 6:00. Besides being home from work and smelling supper on the stove, this is the half hour that *The Andy Griffith Show* comes on. Everything about this classic show is, well...classic. From that contagious theme song that is whistled over scenes of a middle-aged father holding a fishing pole while his son throws rocks down a country road, to the perfectly wrapped morals that help make Mayberry a better place, these thirty minutes have successfully earned a place in the hearts of all Americans, in all walks of life.

The Andy Griffith Show's popularity and episodes have made their way into every TV enthusiast's conversation, second only to today's weather forecast. The brilliance of the writing was very simple; everything they said and did was relatable to people's lives. It was like a perfect country song on film. Real situations and problems about real people. Now to me, *this* is reality TV! Nobody eating worms, or cut-throat job interviews, or blind-date matchmaking, or six different cultures living in one house. Just a laid-back sheriff with a bumbling deputy, enjoying homecooked cholesterol-laden food from a pizzlesprung Aunt, bouncing through the subtle ups and downs of life while raising a good-hearted runny-nosed kid. If this isn't the real deal, then a squirrel ain't got a climbing gear!

And this is one of the few television shows that I'm never bored with or get tired of seeing the reruns. That's a sure-fire sign that something is good. I can quote lines that are coming up after the next commercial or will know what song Andy's going to play on the guitar when he's sitting on the front porch. It doesn't matter, I'm still watching and waiting with the same anticipation as the first time.

But the characters, as I mentioned earlier, are so darn relatable. They each have their own unique attitudes and characteristics, and one of a kind approach to handling certain predicaments. All of this is done, by the way, with a homey humorous slant. I'm laughing right now thinking of Barney dressed up as a bride about to take his vows beside an oak tree! You know the one I'm talking about.

And that's another thing, as soon as you think you know which episode is your favorite, somebody reminds you of another one that makes you second guess your first choice. So which one is your favorite? Opie and the bird? Mr. McBeevy? Aunt Bee's pickles? Barney in the choir? Barney reciting The Preamble? Or the ones with Ernest T. Bass? Or the Darlings? (Now them boys can pick and grin!) I'm partial to any of them with Floyd. Like when Floyd is sitting in his barber chair talking with Andy:

> *Floyd*: Just like Calvin Coolidge said, everybody complains about the weather but no one does anything about it.
> *Andy*: Floyd, I don't think that was Calvin Coolidge who said that. It was Mark Twain.
> *Floyd*: Oh. Well then what did Calvin Coolidge say?

This guy makes me laugh! Oh well, I could fill three pages recalling my favorites. See, I can't even tell you mine.

And along with the humor and storylines, the show was rich with music as well. I mentioned earlier the

Darlings, in real life, the Dillards, who were a bonafide top-notch bluegrass group with albums of their own. And where else can you find a sheriff playing a country guitar with a deputy and a drunkard singing part on a gospel song through the bars of a jail cell? Beautiful! And I dare you to find me one person in the country who can't whistle the theme song. Its popularity is right up there with *Jeopardy*'s.

Let me wrap up with a story that says it all. We all know that when the show went to color, Barney was out, Howard was in and it just wasn't the same. Still good but not great like before. So every Sunday morning, our local channel would run *The Andy Griffith Show* at 10:00; the same time church was starting. My dad, mom, brother and me are in the car turning into the church parking lot one Sunday morning. My dad comments that the lot is fuller than usual and it seems that a lot of people are at church. My brother chimes in, "Must be a color *Andy* on this morning."

THIS MONEY STILL WORKS, DOESN'T IT?

So let me tell you about a couple of things that happened to me the other day. And I tell you because I think of myself as a fairly straightforward kind of guy because I recognize, appreciate and salute the little things throughout the day that contribute to a beautiful way of life. I also believe that to know love, you must know hate; to go up, you must come down; there's black and white, dark and light; you get my drift.

I was on the interstate traveling back home from a work trip and my fuel light obnoxiously told me I needed gas. I got off the next exit and made my way to the outside pump island. I unscrewed the gas cap, put the nozzle in and flipped the pump on. Nothing. Nada. While anxiously pumping the nozzle trigger, I read in bold red letters: YOU MUST PAY FIRST BEFORE PUMP IS ACTIVATED. What? Prepay? I walked in and the clerk had her hand out waiting for me to fork it over.

"Here's $20. I want to fill it up. I'll come back in and pay the rest once it's full."

"Sorry sir. Whatever you give me is the limit I set the pump at. And that big truck of yours is going to take a lot more than $20."

"So I have to pay you first 'cause you don't trust me? And you want me to give you $80 and what I don't use up you'll give my remaining money back? So why should I trust you?"

167

She didn't have an answer because it didn't matter. She "won" because that's the way it works. I gave her $80, got $55 worth of fuel and then, gladly, my $25 back. But before I walked out, I told her this. "I'm from a good country town. Let me explain what this means. When you go to the grocery store, do you first give the cashier $100 and then go shopping? How about when you go to the Tractor Supply Company, do you hand them $100 and then browse the store and they give you your unspent money back? Don't get me wrong, I understand the reason for your own security and fuel theft measures, but it isn't right. I'm one of the good guys, just like most of the gas-users out there. But some jerk fills up and drives off, sticking the station for $50 and now *I* can't be trusted. I'm not upset with you, but I'm disappointed in that we both fall victim to the system. It isn't right."

The next morning, I met a friend for a relaxing round of golf. I'm not that good but I do like to relax! The sun breaking through the clouds was telling me what a great day it was going to be. I walked up to the counter in the Country Club Pro Shop (of which I'm not a member). I handed the 'pro' a $50 bill.

"Sorry bud, we don't take cash. Just credit cards."

"Is this a joke?" You can imagine what look I had on my face.

"No, we're only allowed to accept credit cards."

"And why?"

"Because we've had some trouble with some staff pocketing some cash, so to solve this, we only take credit cards."

Now there are so many things wrong with this picture.

1) I haven't stolen anybody's money---for Pete's sake, I'm trying to give it to you!

2) I'm being punished for being a 'cash man' because I refuse to fall prey to the mentality of a credit card nation.

3) Instead of addressing the actual problem of hiring untrustworthy employees, they've decided to solve this by inconveniencing the very customers who give them the cash to steal. Absurd!

4) And finally, I'm holding real hard cold cash. Alexander Hamilton called it "legal tender." I'm pretty sure it's against the law to not accept cash. And if I'm wrong, well, then it should be a law.

I had to use these two places of business and their inconvenient "nontransaction" policies to let you know how much I appreciate all the other business that don't work this way. Thank you.

Hey, presidential candidates, here's a new brilliant platform for you: Businesses will provide a service and then you pay them for it! And whoever that candidate's going to be, then I'd like to be Secretary of the Treasury. And the first law that I'm going to pass is that everybody everywhere has *got* to accept cash!

TEBOW-MANIA

Tebow. You know who I'm talking about. 24 year old Heisman Trophy winner for Florida. Quarterback for Denver. Devout Christian. And oh yeah, latest target for the mainstream media. Even for this column---not a target though, simply the subject.

As an athlete, he's got the makings. He's competitive, he's committed to putting 100% of his heart into the game, earned his starting position and proved he could and should keep it. His intense workouts make P90X look elementary. On the field and on Sundays, you either love him or hate him. Root for him hard or root against him even harder. That's what being a good athlete is about; when you have as many people rooting against you as you do for you. And that's what sports are about.

But Tebow has transcended the field. His impenetrable character drives nagging postgame reporters crazy. They can't trap him in dogging out other players or teams. They can't find that nick in his persona that they can get their fingernails in and eventually scratch until it's a good size hole. And they can't seem to ruffle his feathers. It's not his style. He smiles, talks about what is good about the progress of he and his team and goes on.

So, there's got to be something they can find to dig at this guy. First it was the eyeblack. In 2010, the NCAA passed "The Tebow Rule" which banned players from writing messages in their eyeblack. He often would put the verse of his chosen scripture from the Bible in his eyeblack. John 3:16. Philippians 4:13. Yeah, I'm sure the defensive linemen were horribly offended at this gesture and couldn't concentrate on playing the game. Sure, that's probably why it got banned.

Since getting a rule named after him, his name then became a verb with the "Tebowing" trend. Mostly it happens on the sidelines, where he drops to one knee, bows his head, a la The Thinker pose, and quietly prays to himself. The Tebowing trend caught like wildfire. Kids everywhere were dropping to one knee and doing their own Tebowing. Good for them! I like to see a wholesome healthy trend catch on for once. It's better than gauge piercings and back tattoos.

But for some reason, when someone is getting a lot of attention for doing good in their lives, that ever-present human skeptical nature perks up and asks "is this guy for real?" So if you've asked this question or subscribe to Bill Maher's newsletter, here are few things to know. I mean, let's face it, there hasn't been this many people following a white Bronco since O.J got arrested.

Every game, Tim chooses someone who is suffering or dying and flies them to the game, rents a limo for him or her and their family, visits with them before the game, gets them 30 yard line tickets, buys their dinner, and then visits for an hour with them after his postgame interviews. Home or away. Every game.

Before he sends the family home with gifts, he always prays with them his own secret prayer for people in their condition. He says he never completely understands why they feel so inspired by his gestures; he says he is the one who is inspired by just getting the opportunity to spend time with these fighters of life and keepers of faith.

I'm not saying that I'm now a die-hard Denver fan. All my blue and orange shirts have sabres on them. But in the world of some crazy headlines that we live in with people and stories like Kardashians, reality show premises, and why meat is bad for you, how refreshing to read about someone who is the real deal. Right down to the fact that Tebow doesn't drink for fear that kids might use that as an excuse to try alcohol. To believe in someone who says, "...in the end, the thing I most want to do is not win championships or make a lot of money, it's to invest in people's lives, to make a difference."

Okay, so maybe I did order a #15 blue and orange jersey.

INFOMERCIALS

I'm not Catholic, but I feel I need to confess an unwritten "sin" that I seem to keep committing. Okay, maybe not a "sin," but something I've consistently done that I'm not all that proud of. Yes, I admit it, I'm a sucker for an infomercial. Call it weak, naïve, hopeful...I don't care what you call it, I just know that I'm an easy sale and here's my credit card number. And I don't care about cheap sets, bad lighting, and cheesy overacting, either. Bring it on!

Now CD packages are my biggest weakness. Being a music lover, it's safe to say that my iPod runneth over with melodious inventory. But if you hire an 80's one-hit wonder with some outdated power ballad hair, and package 40 great songs that I may already own with a new flashy cover, I'll bite harder than Mike Tyson on Holyfield's ear.

That Hampton Inn notepad in the top drawer of my nightstand is filled with 1-800 numbers of the latest and greatest and best new reasonably priced deals with three easy payments, just waiting to make my life simpler, easier, and healthier. I know it's 90% plastic and will probably break after its third use, but I'm a gamblin' man and I still have a little room left in the junk drawer. If it's a juicer, a shooter, a peeler, a masher, a twister---basically any transitive verb with an *er* ending---I'm sold.

I completely realize that there is an entire room in my basement that is dedicated to all those fantastic infomercial buys. There's the Ab-Scruncher, a box full of

Clappers, the Bacon Genie, Dust Mop Slippers, a case full of Oxi-Clean, and a DVD box set of Soul Train. You just never know when you might need something like this.

The latest purchase was the energizing magnet bracelet. A stylish piece of magnetic and rubberized jewelry that supplies me with more energy and will improve my balance? Send me two for each wrist! I can't honestly say that my energy level has soared through the roof, but I have yet to fall down stairs and I can stand on one leg for almost four seconds. I can justify some results somewhere in there, can't I?

I'm thinking about inventing the Infomercial Blocker 4000. (You always have to put a big number after the product name---it makes it sound that much more powerful and able to do the job! Plus you can charge more.) This product will attach to your tv and block all the infomercials from 1 am-5:30am. But my dilemma is that I have to advertise and sell it in an infomercial and then I'd wind up blocking my own sales! Never mind...on to the Doggie Doorbell 2800 idea.

P.T. Barnum was once famously quoted for saying, "There's a sucker born every minute." Well, I was born 30 odd years ago and I am still going strong!

MISNOMERS

The English language is a pretty crazy thing. There are antonyms, synonyms, homonyms, M&Ms, antecedents that should never disagree, and even participles that sometimes dangle. It's been reported at times that English is the most difficult language to learn. However, aside from the Language of Love, it's the most used and understood one there is. Most of us learn and master it to the ability that we can communicate accurately to one another.

But one thing I don't get is how something gets to be termed something that it is not. It doesn't make any sense. We call them misnomers. As if the English language isn't hard enough, we had to go and make it even harder. And I'm not talking about how a starfish is not really a fish, or why you drive on a parkway and park in a driveway, or even that quicksand works so slow. I'm talking about some bigger ones. Like why the New York Jets and Giants play in New Jersey. And why the Scotland Yard is in England. And why Greenland is icy and Iceland is greener. Well, here are a few more that have been "misnomed."

The Black Box: The flight data recorder, or more commonly known as the Black Box, holds vital information for the aircraft's flight and activity. However, it's not black; it's bright orange. It's painted orange for rescuers to find it more easily. We call it a "black" box because, well…the jury's still out on that one.

Chinese Checkers: Everyone's played the six-pointed board game with hopping marbles. Got news for you, though: it neither originated in China, or any part of Asia for that matter, and it's not in the "checker" family. It's closer to marbles and it came from Germany.

You can catch a cold going outside with a wet head: Mothers all across the planet secretly joined hands and agreed on this one. There are still things to learn about the common cold, but the fact that wet heads will cause them is not so. If you go outside with a wet head, the only thing you'll have is a cold wet head! (Okay, so maybe this is more a myth than a misnomer, but I had to include it.)

Big Ten / PAC 10 / Big 12: College football is big sports business! You really just need to know that UVA and VT are in the ACC and nobody understands how the BCS rankings work. Big 10, PAC 10, and the Big 12 are 3 major conferences in college football. Here's where it gets confusing and just downright silly. In 2011, there will be 12 teams in the Big 10, 12 teams in the PAC 10, and 10 teams in the Big 12. TCU, located in Texas, will join the Big East. And I Don't Know is on third!

Foods: Lots of misnomers in the food world. Boston cream pie is actually a cake. There's no ham in a hamburger. The breakfast cereal Grape-Nuts has neither grapes or nuts in it. London broil is a North American dish; they apparently don't know about it in London. And contrary to what my kids once thought, Hush Puppies is not "quiet dog meat"; just little breaded nuggets of fatty goodness!

And oh yeah, one more. Isn't the word misnomer a misnomer? I mean, shouldn't it be mis*namer*?

MAW MAW LEFT THE LIGHT ON

My grandmother, or Maw Maw as I called her, was definitely a different kind of bird.

Before she'd say something that she knew the rest of the family would scrunch their faces at, she'd give me that crooked grin and a wink that said *get ready and watch this.*

Example: I remember the time when the rates on everybody's electric bill went up quite a smart bit. It really made people think twice about leaving a lamp on in a room that they weren't in. One time before me, my mom and brother and Maw Maw were going to the mall, Maw Maw went back inside and turned a few lamps on before we left. My mom, obviously confused, asked, "You've been complaining about the electric company raising their rates, then why do you leave lights on all the time now?" Maw Maw never skipped a beat. "If they're going to raise their prices, then I'm going to get my money's worth!"

Or how about this one. Keep in mind that Maw Maw was so stubborn at times, she'd make a ten year old mule blush with envy. One visit on a Sunday afternoon at my grandparents' house, the subject turned to religion. Paw Paw, who read his Bible three times a day, was teaching me the lesson of forgiveness by telling me that the Bible says we should forgive our enemies seventy times seven. Maw Maw bristled a bit and declared, "That's not in the Bible." After I retrieved Paw Paw's Bible for him, he showed us where this verse was. And then Maw Maw closed it up, pointed to the inscription on the front that read his embossed personalized name. Then with a quick emphatic nod, she said, "Well no wonder. But that verse ain't in *my* Bible!"

Okay then, I'll leave you with this one. It should be no surprise to you to learn that Maw Maw was also very superstitious. And not just the "don't walk under ladders" and "black cats crossing your path." She knew them all. And one in particular that I was never aware of until this peculiar happening. One of Maw Maw's neighbors down the road became pregnant. She would take her food and check in on her from time to time and make sure this expectant mother was taking care of herself and her 'belly baby'. And she would also warn her to make sure not to do anything to "mark" her baby before birth. Yes, Maw Maw believed that a mother could determine, or I guess more appropriately, *pre*determine certain characteristics in a child's formative and developing stages. Like listening to loud rock music would make the little one wild or climbing ladders while pregnant would cause the baby to be scared of heights. Well, fate intervened one day while this woman was in her seventh month of pregnancy. While driving to the store, she hit a horse in the road. It proved to be a minor accident as all three who were involved were thankfully unharmed. But a few months later, Maw Maw visited the mother and her three day old beautiful and healthy son. And upon seeing the little fellow for the first time, Maw Maw boldly said, "I knew it. That boy looks just like a horse right in the face!"

I treasure her memories and stories every day; especially when I leave home and see that I've left a lamp on!

GUITAR LESSONS

I play the guitar. To some novice players, I guess I might rank as being pretty good. To a lot of other seasoned players, I'm probably viewed as not knowing too much past page 6 in a Mel Bay instructional book.

No matter how good you are, one thing is for sure: when you play that first song all the way through with no mistakes and hit all the notes, it is absolute unexplainable satisfaction. Much like that feeling one gets hitting his first home run, or seeing that A+ at the top of your first book report, or when your mother-in-law asks you for the recipe of the dish you just made for dinner. Complete accomplishment.

Me and my guitar have become pretty good friends over the years. She's helped me figure out what notes to hit --- and in which order --- to make a melody come alive to have the ultimate effect to a listener. She sometimes gets a little flat or a little sharp, which reminds me to not take advantage of her or expect too much from her and to give her the attention to tune her up so she can perform her best and live up to her part of our partnership. I learned a lot from her and when we both work together, we can, literally and figuratively, make music in harmony.

The reason I began to even play the guitar started on a summer day when I was 12 years old. I was sitting at my dad's desk pretending to be a responsible adult and do some much-needed deskwork. Among playing with the letter opener, a paperweight and a legal pad, I found an old eight-track sitting on top of the stereo. Yes, I said eight-track! I put it in the player to have some background music to "work" by. The third song grabbed my ears and wouldn't let go. It was an instrumental titled "The Entertainer." It was played on the guitar by some guy named Chet Atkins. I had no idea who he was but my youthful musical detector felt that he wasn't too shabby and when he played it, it sounded like four guitars playing at once!

I decided right then and there that I would be happy to spend the rest of my life trying to make the guitar sound just a fraction as good as he made it sound. I soon realized that this Chet Atkins carried the honorable title of "Godfather of the Guitar" and is still today arguably the best guitarist to ever live.

A few years ago, I spent some time with a friend who knew Mr. Atkins personally, and he shared some stories with me about him. One in particular applies to my life every day.

He told me Chet was in the studio and another guitar player was on the session that day, also. Trying to impress "The Man," the younger guitar player got Mr. Atkins' attention and pointed to a brand-new shiny guitar in it's newly purchased tortoise shell satin-lined case. "I just bought that six string axe there for $1500. And Chet, that is one of the best sounding guitars you'll ever hear."

Chet turned and looked at it and said, "Really?" He then stared at it in complete silence for an uncomfortable 20 seconds. He looked back to the other player and politely uttered, "Hmmmm....I don't hear a thing."

The proud owner, with a blushed face, quickly realized that that piece of wood is nothing without the player. Lesson learned.

It was a modern-day parable of the old wise saying, "it's not the arrows, it's the Indians." That piece of wood sitting in the corner reminds me that it will only sound as good as I make it. I have to apply myself to see any kind of result. And you will only get out of something whatever you put into it.

I might take 10,000 more lessons to learn how to play like Chet Atkins, but none will ever teach as much as this "guitar lesson."

MORE ABOUT THE WRITER

Langdon Reid has used his multiple writing talents to find success in various fields. Not only did he write this book, he is one-half the country music duo, Wilson Fairchild. Langdon has been performing and writing music since he was fourteen years old. He has had over 30 of his songs recorded by an assortment of artists in the country, bluegrass, and gospel fields, and has had freelance columns and articles published in numerous newspapers and magazines. Langdon is the co-author of a Christmas book, *You Know It's Christmas When...* with his father, Don and brother, Debo. He then co-authored another book, *Andy Wouldn't Let Me*, with friend and writer, Bryan Kennedy. He is also an accomplished guitarist and vocalist.

Langdon serves an elder and Sunday school teacher in his home church, Olivet Presbyterian. He lives with his wife, Alexis, and two children, Caroline and Davis, in Staunton, Virginia in the heart of the beautiful Shenandoah Valley.

Be sure to follow Langdon on Twitter & Facebook.

But please don't follow him in the car...he really hates tailgaters.

185